D1379470

Augel's

YOUNG LEONARDO

BiG

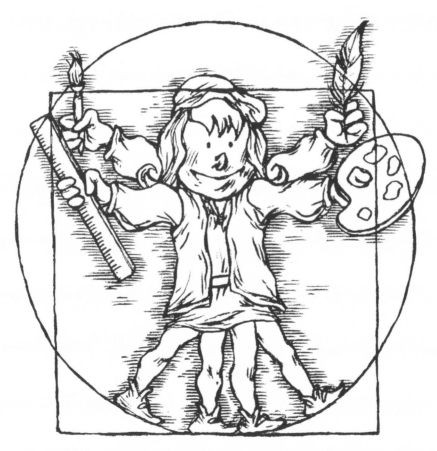

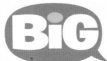

WILLIAM AUGEL
Story & Art

•

BENJAMIN CROZE
Translator

•

**AMANDA LUCIDO &
FABRICE SAPOLSKY**
US Edition Editors

HARLEY SALBACKA
Additional Activities

VINCENT HENRY
Original Edition Editor

JERRY FRISSEN
Senior Art Director

RYAN LEWIS
Junior Designer

MARK WAID
Publisher

Rights and Licensing - licensing@humanoids.com
Press and Social Media - pr@humanoids.com

YOUNG LEONARDO. This title is a publication of Humanoids, Inc. 8033 Sunset Blvd. #628, Los Angeles, CA 90046.
Copyright © 2021 Humanoids, Inc., Los Angeles (USA). All rights reserved. Humanoids and its logos are ® and © 2021 Humanoids, Inc.
Library of Congress Control Number: 2020903455

B+G is an imprint of Humanoids, Inc.

First published in France under the title "Le petit Léonard de Vinci" Copyright © 2020 La Boîte à Bulles & William Augel. All rights reserved.
All characters, the distinctive likenesses thereof and all related indicia are trademarks of La Boîte à Bulles Sarl and/or of William Augel.

No portion of this book may be reproduced by any means without the express written consent
of the copyright holder except for artwork used for review purposes. Printed in Latvia.

La Famiglia

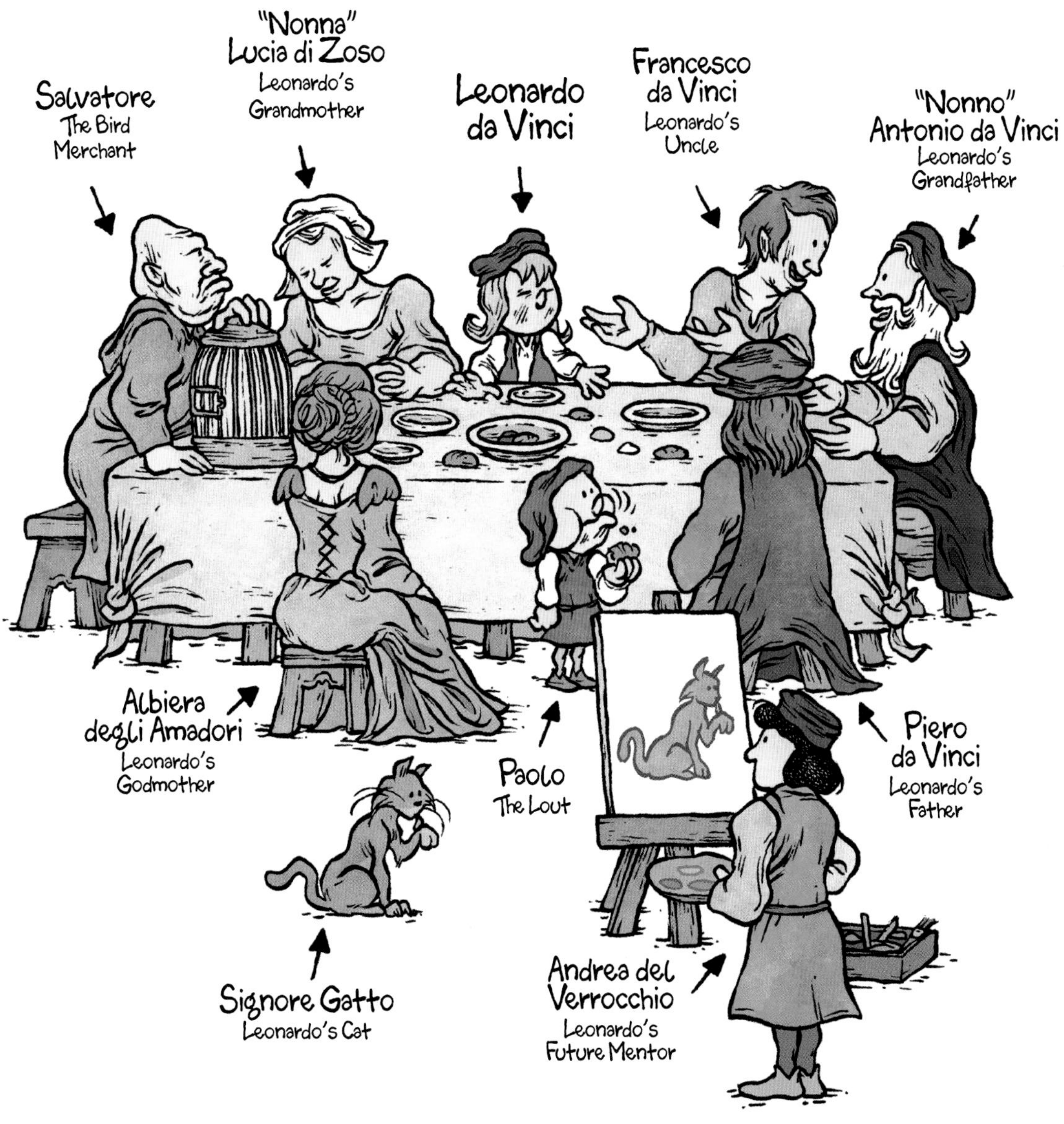

"Nonna"
Lucia di Zoso
Leonardo's
Grandmother
Salvatore
The Bird
Merchant
Leonardo
da Vinci
Francesco
da Vinci
Leonardo's
Uncle
"Nonno"
Antonio da Vinci
Leonardo's
Grandfather
Albiera
degli Amadori
Leonardo's
Godmother
Paolo
The Lout
Piero
da Vinci
Leonardo's
Father
Signore Gatto
Leonardo's Cat
Andrea del
Verrocchio
Leonardo's
Future Mentor

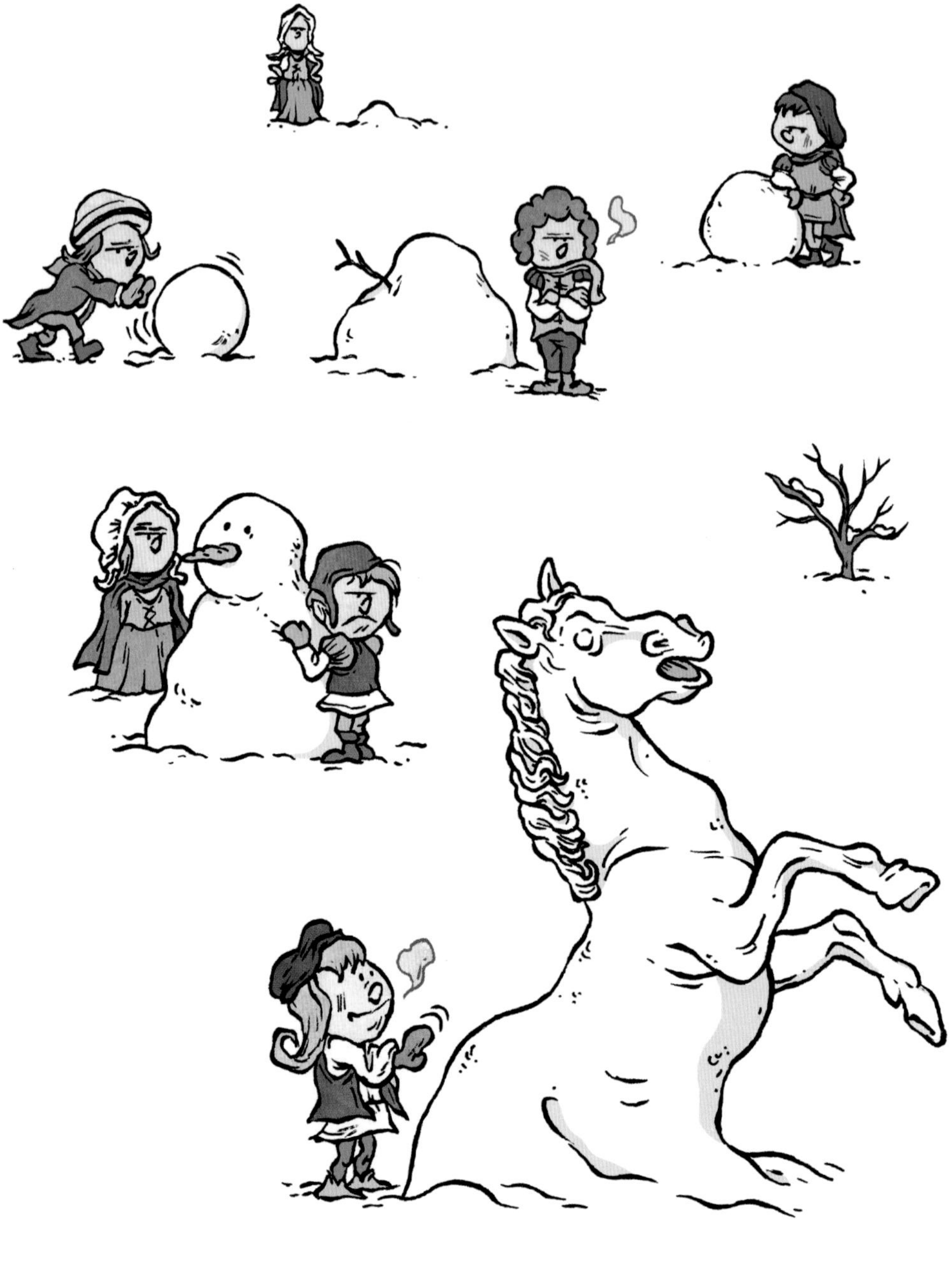

Snow Angels

 What are you doing lying down in the snow? You're gonna catch a cold...

 Have you ever made a snow angel?

 Snow angel? I'll show you!

yippeeeeee!!!

And there you have it! What d'ya think?

Isn't it fascinating how the human body can fit... ...into a circle? Now let's try a square... Perfect fit!

Man is the *ideal* geometric model! I mean... Your angel is lovely...?

Andrea del Verrocchio

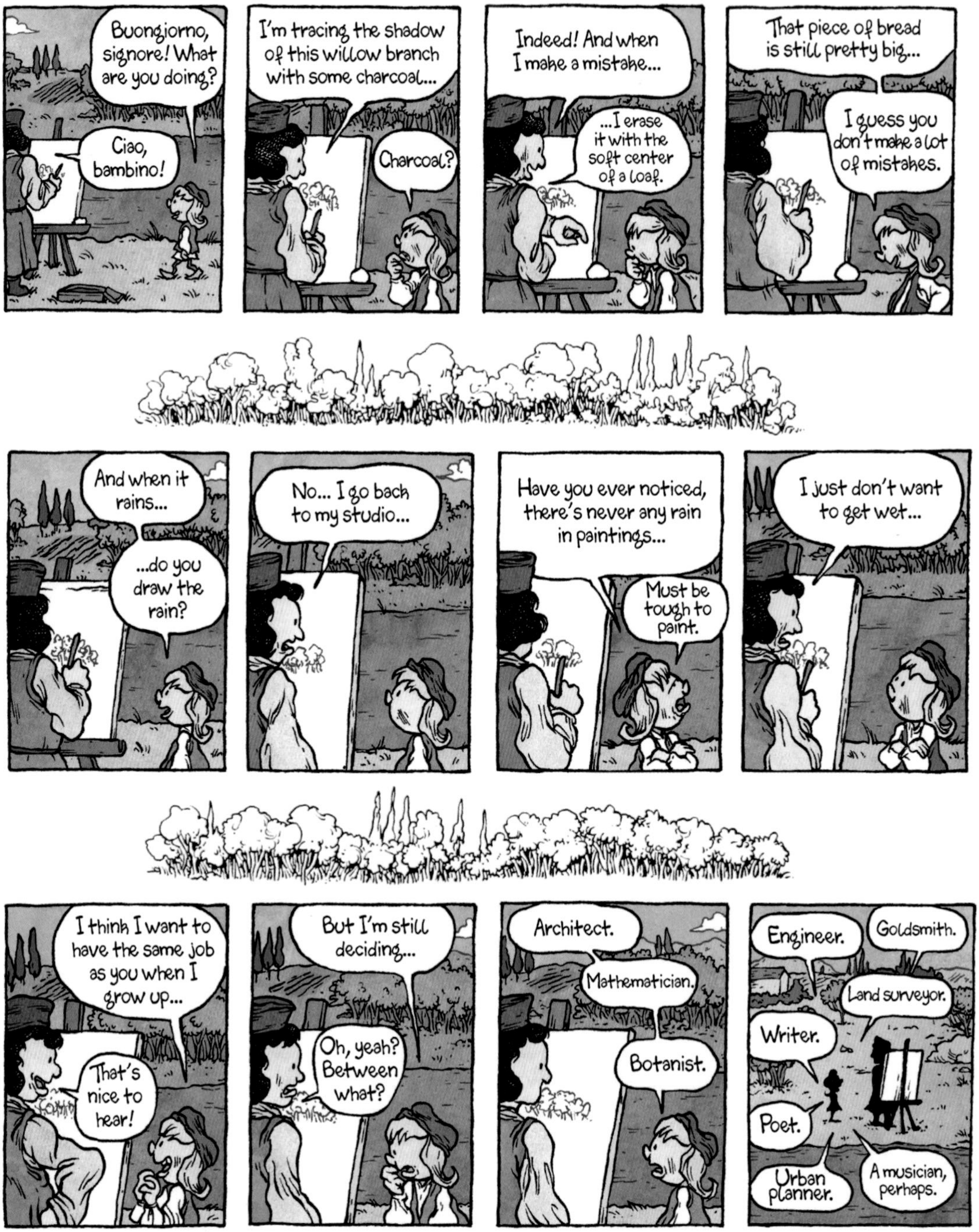

Buongiorno, signore! What are you doing?
Ciao, bambino!
I'm tracing the shadow of this willow branch with some charcoal...
Charcoal?
Indeed! And when I make a mistake...
...I erase it with the soft center of a loaf.
That piece of bread is still pretty big...
I guess you don't make a lot of mistakes.
And when it rains...
...do you draw the rain?
No... I go back to my studio...
Have you ever noticed, there's never any rain in paintings...
Must be tough to paint.
I just don't want to get wet...
I think I want to have the same job as you when I grow up...
That's nice to hear!
But I'm still deciding...
Oh, yeah? Between what?
Architect.
Mathematician.
Botanist.
Engineer.
Goldsmith.
Land surveyor.
Writer.
Poet.
Urban planner.
A musician, perhaps.

Inspiration

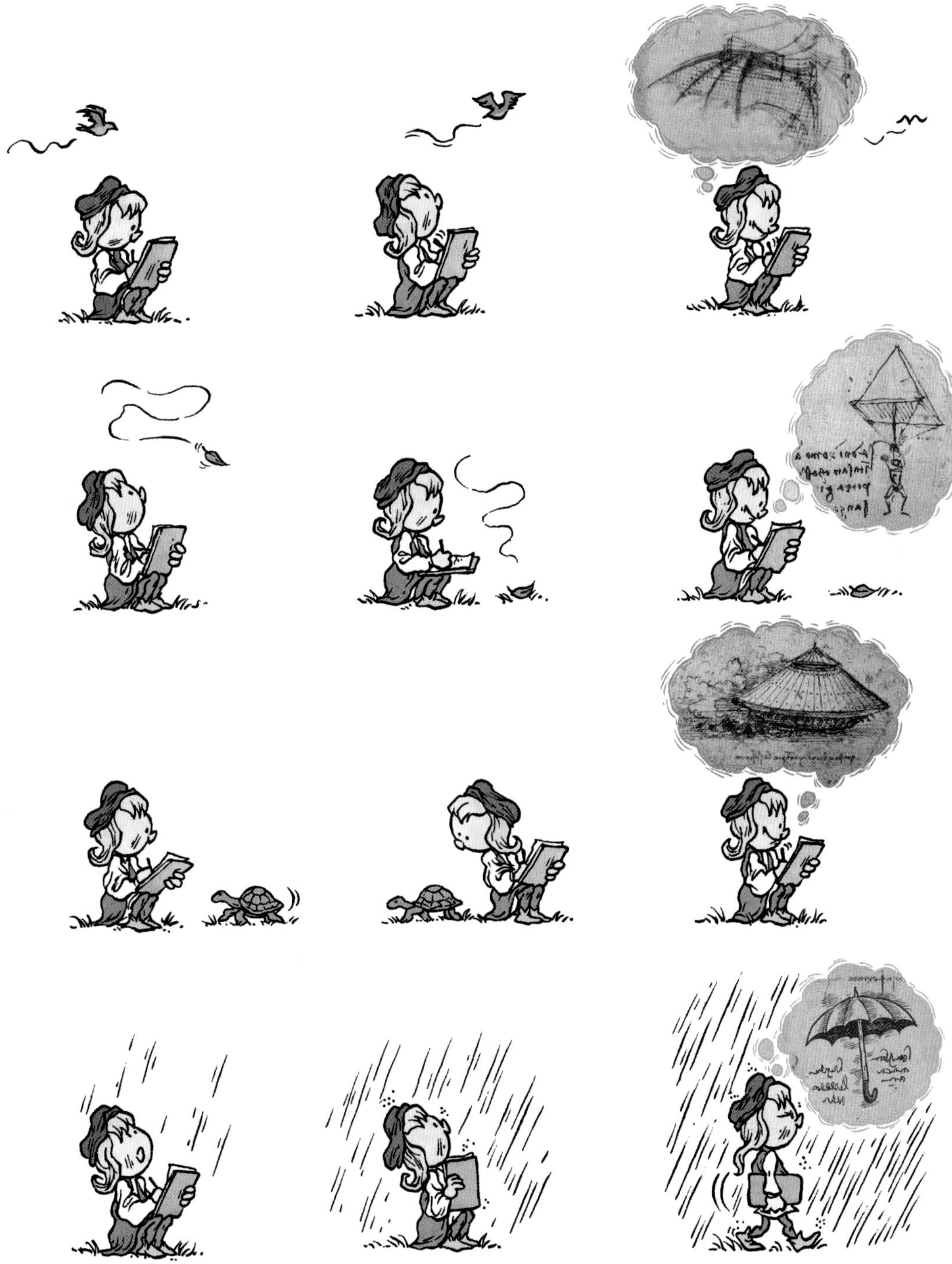

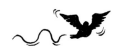

Are you working on your crane project?

Nah... I ditched the crane for a bridge...

So you're working on the bridge then?

Nope, I decided to draw a dragon...

But come to think of it, I'd rather draw a landscape...

You suffer from procrastination, my boy!

Pro... Procra...

Is that... a *serious* condition?

It just means that you keep putting everything off till later...

Oh, all right...

What a dreadful word!

Leo, your room isn't going to clean *itself!*

Maybe later, you know I can't right now...

...I have a condition...

Signore Gatto

The... The mouse...
It's... it's...

Monstruoso!

Bad
kitty!

Scritch!
Scritch!

scritch!

CRASH!

Leo, did you break
something?

It was
the cat!

I have
proof!

Scritch!
Scritch!

Scritch!

da Vinci Code

What's with the strange handwriting?

I'm writing backward to code my notes...

That way my research can stay secret!

I'm a genius!

Are you aware that any *ordinary mirror* can decipher your *ingenious ploy?*

If you can read this, don't!

You're writing with your *left* hand now?

I write better with this hand, and it's easier for writing backwards.

Are all those spelling mistakes *also* meant to *confuse* the reader?

Obviously...

If you can read this, mind your own business!

Maybe the backward thing wasn't such a good idea after all...

I have no idea what I wrote...

Shadow Puppets

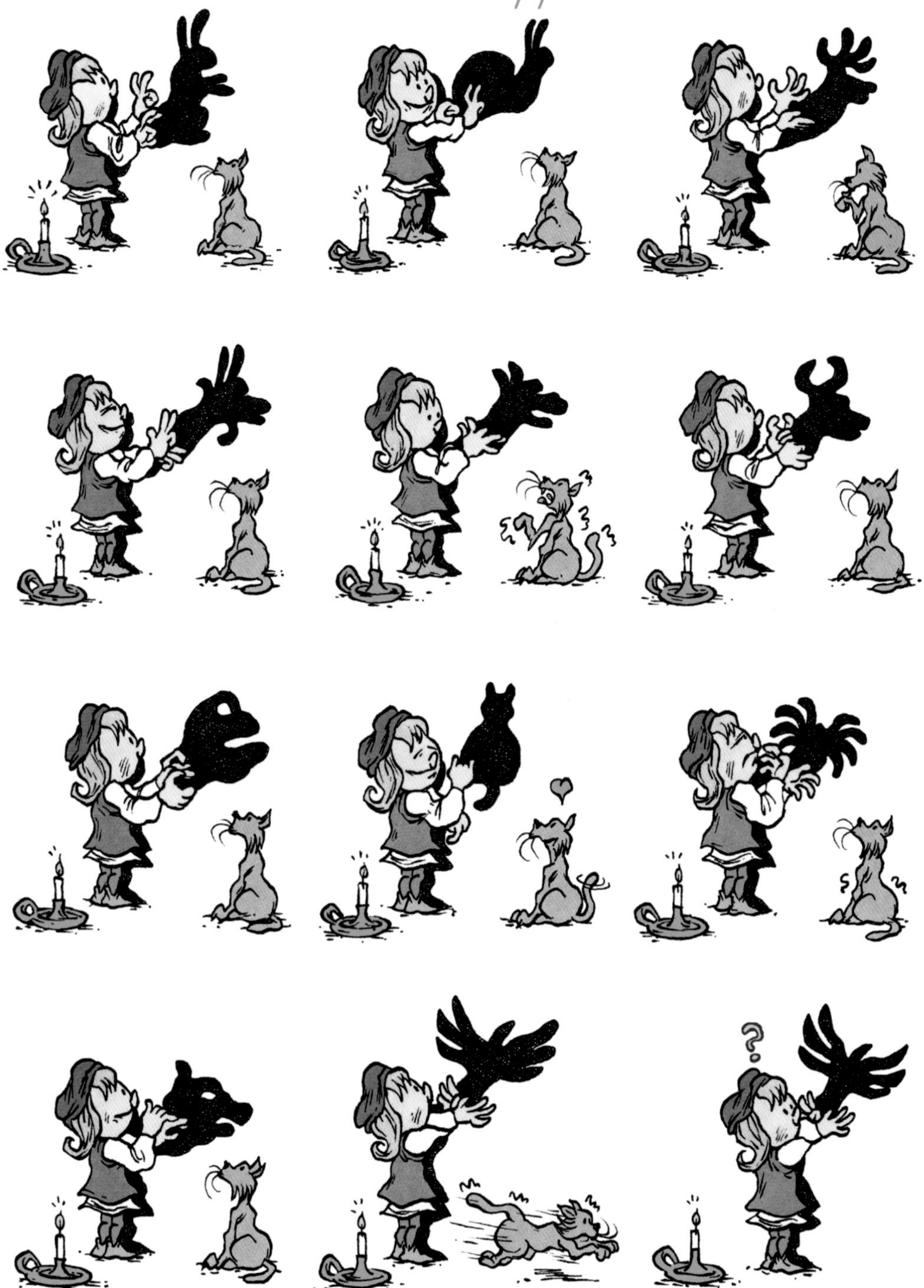

Bandito

I put a lock on the cage just for you!

You think you can set the birds free when I'm not looking, eh?

A double-locking padlock and cylinder with three multidirectional cotter pins...

Really?

Are you kidding?

Free the birds and I'll draw your portrait...

How 'bout it?

Well, you do have a reputation for drawing very well...

Okay, deal! Make me look good!

That'll cost extra...

I'll do it for three birds!

Strike a pose, show me your good side!

Like this?

Perfect!

Turn a little more to your left!

You sure?

Yes, yes.

But...you're only going to see my back--

scritch

You thief!

Three denarii per bird. No denarii, no bird!

It's as simple as that!

I just figured that since I'm only a poor kid and all...

...you could give me a deal!

A deal, sure...

Scram!

Poor little creatures, frightened and crammed together...

...knowing they won't soar through the blue sky ever again...

Yeah, it's terrible...

I didn't realize you cared so much for them...

Poverino...

Now I have to raise the prices really high...

That's weird, you didn't try to free my birds...

...this time!

As a matter of fact, they've stopped chirping...

Hm...

A painting, an illusion!

My birds!

Bandito!

...!

13

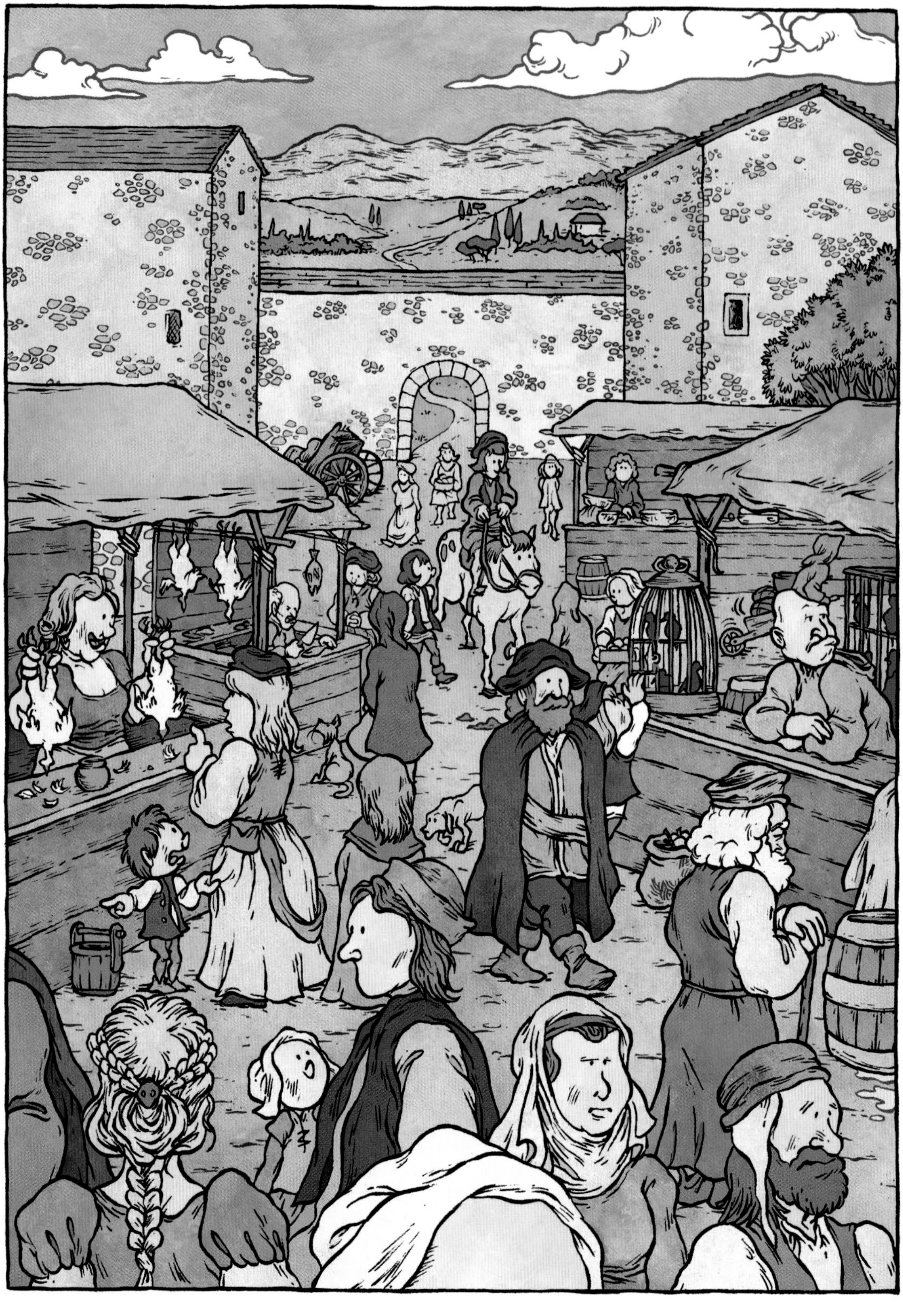

The Butterfly

You look as cute as a butterfly, Goldilocks!

Is it carnival?

Ha ha!

Ignoramus!

Take a good look, because I'm about to...fly!

Wee!

Baf!

I've never seen a butterfly turn into a caterpillar before...

Urg...

Buongiorno, Leo!

Buongiorno Nonno!

Be a good boy and join your grandfather for a stroll...

Still keeping your eyes open, I hope?

Always!

I'm working on a device that will allow me to fly!

Very well...

Where do you plan to do your test flights?

The top of a cliff, of course!

This all sounds very dangerous to me...

Don't worry!

Tell me, Leo, do you know the story of Icarus?

You mean the grocer?

No, no, no. Let me tell you his story...

Icarus and his father Daedalus were prisoners of King Minos. To escape him, Daedalus fashioned wings out of wax and feathers...

Before leaving, Daedalus warned his son not to get too close to the sun because of the heat...

Only, exhilarated by his flight, Icarus flew too close and the wax melted...

His wings broke off and he plummeted...

Daedalus should have turned to bats for inspiration...

Wax...

Feathers, sheesh...

Their patagia are way more adapted...

Duh!

And it would have been wiser to fly out on a cloudy day!

He's nuts!

Apart from these technical aspects, isn't there some other conclusion you can draw from this story?

Definitely! The sun is way too hot...

And Daedalus is an idiot!

17

No Time...

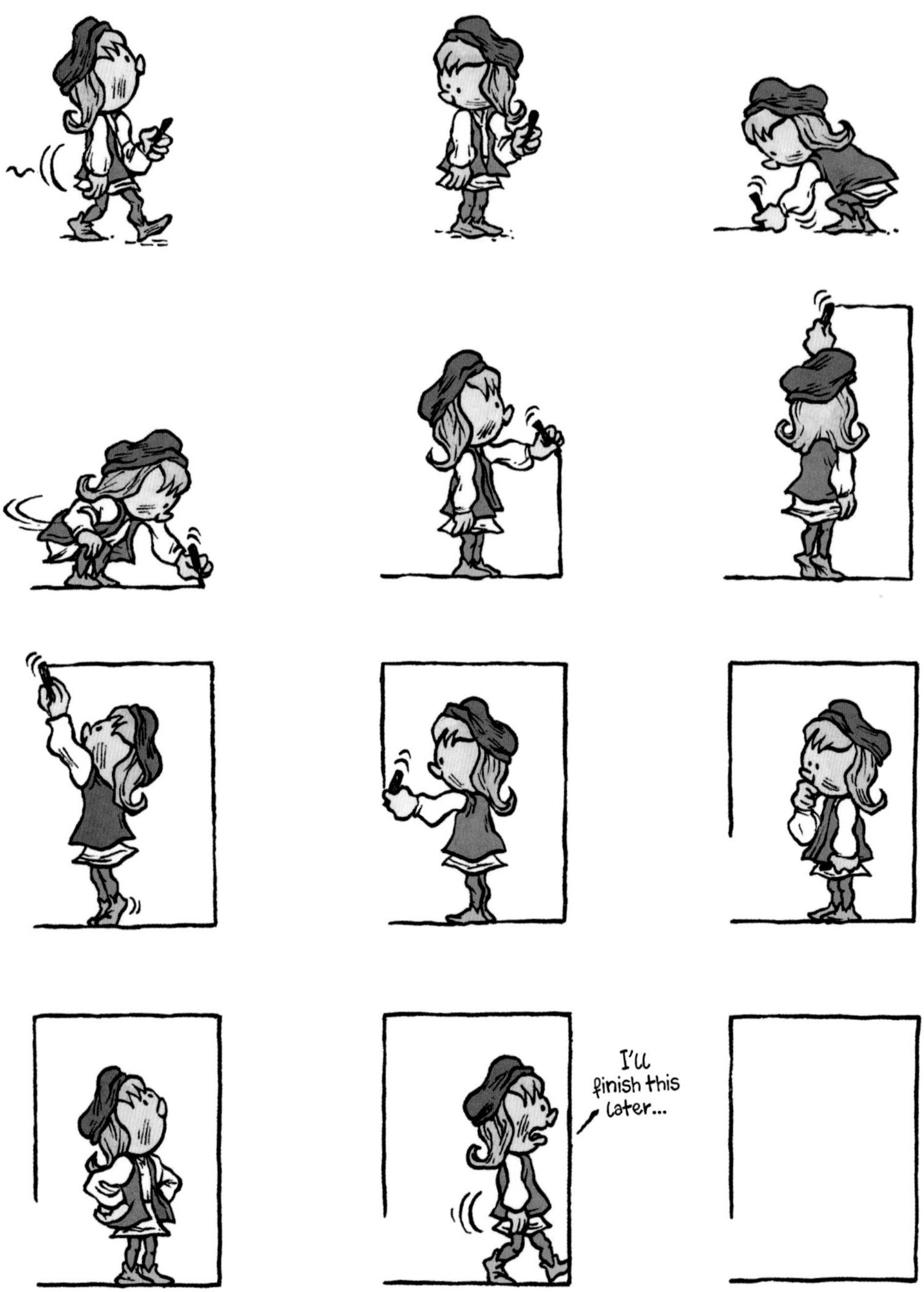
I'll finish this later...

The Roundel

This roundel was meant for a scarecrow...

So I'd like you to paint something scary...

I'm counting on you!

Uh...

Okay, so... what's scarier than my dad?

What in the world is that?

Well...it's a bat...

Can't you tell?

Are you trying to scare the birds or make them laugh? Start over!

I don't get it... they can get caught in your hair...

That's horrid!

I combined several hideous animals...

...here's the result!

Oh my, how dreadful!

You should be ashamed, coming up with such a thing!

But, but...

Good work!

19

You, knowing your errors,
will correct your works, and
where you find mistakes amend
them, and remember never to
fall into them again.

Leonardo

Nonna

Would you like to know the secrets of pottery?

It's basically shaping a spinning lump of clay...

Is there anything else to know?

How would you like to draw pictures on my pottery?

I'd love to!

I already have an idea!

I'm gonna draw a dragon attaching a lion!

Little flowers will do just fine...

With a dragon?

Just flowers!

Pff...

I sketched some violets, what do you think?

That's beautiful but... I was thinking of something a bit simpler..

Such as?

A circle with petals around it, for instance...

A circle with...

I don't get it.

Oh no... there's a fly in...

Gotcha! I painted that fly!

Hehe!

Good one, but now you have to remove it...

Why's that?

It's a soup bowl!

And no one wants a fly in their soup...

Why do I have to draw fruit?

Because it's going to be a fruit bowl!

I wonder what I would have drawn...

...if it had been a chamber pot!

Why did you draw a bird on the milk jug?

So that Signore Gatto wouldn't go near it...

The cat?

Yeah, he's afraid of birds...

The Bat Cave

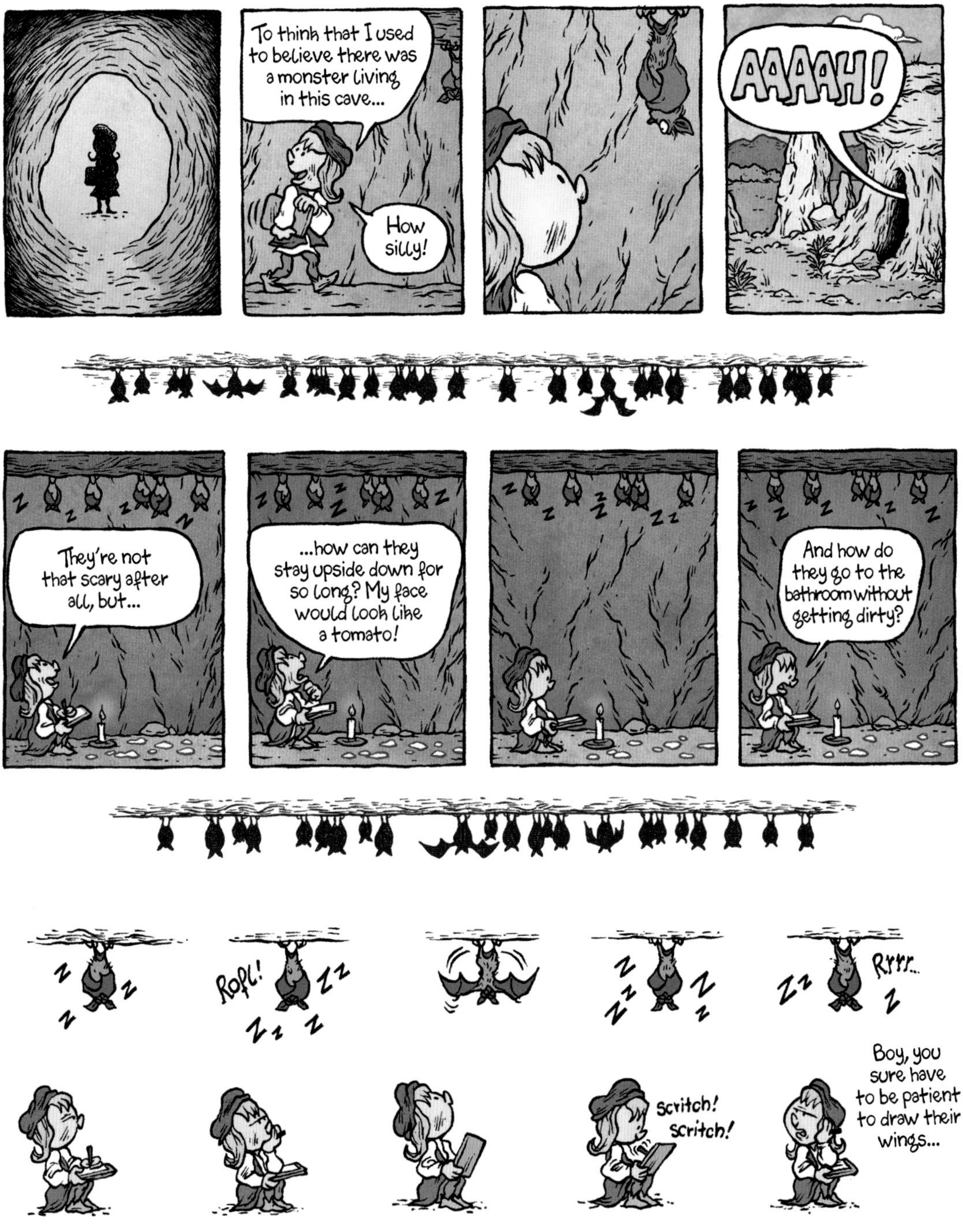

To think that I used to believe there was a monster living in this cave...
How silly!
AAAAH!
They're not that scary after all, but...
...how can they stay upside down for so long? My face would look like a tomato!
And how do they go to the bathroom without getting dirty?
Ropl!
Rrrr...
Scritch! Scritch!
Boy, you sure have to be patient to draw their wings...

The Dragonfly

Dragonflies can fly very fast!

Which is convenient for escaping predators...

Is there such a thing as a giant toad?

Thanks to its two pairs of wings...

...a dragonfly can fly backwards very quickly.

And considering how high this is...

...I may do just that...

Still, I wonder if these two pairs of wings...

...are making me a little too heavy...

Whoah!

I wasn't really expecting an answer!

So how's the portrait coming along?

Fine, fine...

Make me look *handsome* this time, will you?

It's a gift for my fiancée...

Listen, I don't do "handsome," I draw it like I see it.

Oh, look who's here!

Signore Gatto!

Did you know he's afraid of birds?

The cat?

Yes!

Krr...

Let's see, a simple *drawing* of a bird should do the trick...

Ah, voilà!

Kiiiiiish!!

MeoOOOow!!

You know, I think I can make you handsome after all...

Umpf...

The smallest feline
is a masterpiece.

Leonardo

We need you, Goldilocks!

Don't call me that!

We need one more player to play calcio. You in, Goldilocks?

Seriously... can't you think of anything better to do than kick a ball around?

Maybe you'd rather we kick a person... Catch my drift?

Is this the game that involves kicking the ball into the opposite camp...

My favorite part...

...while beating each other up like brutes?

...but no tackling from behind!

Perfect!

Here... I painted the ball!

Not bad, eh?

It's a truncated icosahedron composed of polygons and hexagons...

Bello!

We owe this to Archimedes!

You can thank him!

There's no way I'm thanking him if he's playing for the other team!

27

A Memory

"My earliest memory is from when I was still in the cradle. A vulture came down to me...

"He opened my mouth with his tail and struck me a few times before putting his tailfeathers in my mouth..."

And you remember all of this?

I sure do!

It's a sign, an invitation to dedicate myself to the flight of birds...

What else could it mean?

I have to figure out a way to make Man fly!

It's obvious!

And what if he put his feather in your mouth for some other reason?

Perhaps to keep you quiet...

Pfff...

In any case, you were lucky it was a vulture...

Why's that?

If it had been a chicken...

...you'd be teaching us how to lay eggs!

I'm flying!

I did it!

My dream has come true!

And here's Florence!

Magnificent!

Brunelleschi's dome!

Beautiful!

Hee hee! That cloud looks like Signore Gatto...

Hey, I was just talking about you, but...wait...

You can fly?

That's impossible!

Your presence defies all logic...

Unless...

The Yo-Yo

Look what I have! It's one of the most ancient toys in the world!

Dooown... and back up it goes!

Oooh... Oooh...

I just can't remember what they call it...

Anyone have an idea?

Io!*

Io!*

"Io-Io"?! That's it! It's a Yo-Yo!

*Io: "me" in Italian.

Pretty great what you can do with a Yo-Yo, huh?

squiiiit!

squiiiit!

squiiiit!

Come sit with your Nonno, show me what you're working on...

I've taken an interest in anatomy lately.

I'm drawing animal corpses in detail...

But mind you! Only animals that have died of natural causes...

It would be cruel otherwise...

Look, you can see how the tendons connect the muscles to the bones...

Understanding how the body works is so fascinating...

I agree.

Speaking of anatomy, why don't you draw girls?

Eh?

Girls...

Girls? Yuch! What for?

That's gross!

Look at this one, you can see the mouse's guts...

Ah...

Yes.

What is it?

A bridge!

It's so small...

It's a scale-model of a self-supporting bridge. It can stand without fasteners, screws or glue...

Revolutionary!

Is this a bridge for hedgehogs or something?

I told you, it's a scale-model...

A what?

A miniature version, if you will...

Call it what you want, you still can't walk on it...

'Cause it's a scale-model...

Like you always say, nothing beats a demonstration...

STOP!

There, what did I tell you?

NO!

Way too small!

CRAC!

A word of advice, genius: build a bigger bridge next time!

It's a scale-model!

The Spaghetti

What's this?

My latest invention! It's going to make the longest spaghetti in the world!

Five meters!

Unless the cat gets to it first...

SHOO!

Can I ask you a question?

Yes, of course!

How are you going to put the spaghetti in the pot without breaking it?

Once it dries...

Where are you off to?

To build a five-meter pot!

SLURP!

Can't do that with five-meter-long spaghetti!

Eh?

My giant spaghetti deserves better van vat!

You came?

This means so much to me. Thanks, friends!

It, it... fills me with joy--

We just wanna see you wipe out...

The joy is ours...

Prepare to see me fly...

...for I am the Human Bat!

Who would want to look like a bat?

They're ugly!

I heard daylight makes them crazy...

That explains a lot...

Hey, remember me?!

This is like the twentieth time, I still can't get enough...

Same!

Even if it starts off slow and painful...

He sure talks a lot...

But the end is really worth it!

Yeah, it's...

...smashing!

Ha! You said it!

Aaarg

Life is pretty simple:
You do some stuff. Most fails.
Some works. You do more
of what works...

Leonardo

Baaa!

Baaa! Baaa!
Baaa!

Baaa!

Baaa!

My uncle asked me to look after the sheep...

How exciting...

Baaa!

I tried drawing them to pass the time...

...but I fell asleep...

Ba   aa!

At least I can look at the clouds...

They're like drawings in the sky...

It stimulates the imagination...

Hmm...

Another sheep!

Baaa!

The Catapult

Poc!

What's up?

I'm throwing stones at these figs to get them to fall...

Trying to, at least...

I've got just the thing for you!

Be right back!

Something tells me he isn't getting a ladder...

Too simple for him...

Here you go, I built a mini catapult!

It's made up of two large springs carved out of bentwood...

This allows for better precision and I have, of course, added my artistic touch...

Why are you telling me all this? I'm not going to buy it!

Wanna see a demonstration?

CRASH!

Well done, your catapult is so poorly designed...

...that it decided to self-destruct!

Pigments

Buongiorno, bambino!

Buongiorno, signore!

May I ask you a question?

Certo!

How do you make colors to paint with?

With pigments you get from grinding certain materials...

...and mixing the powder with oil or eggs.

I actually have a little stone with me from which you can extract blue...

Azurite!

Oooh...

Pigments can come from minerals, plants, or even...

...animals!

So you... you grind animals into powder?

You're a MONSTER!

Relax, it's mostly insects, like a hermes, for example...

It's a beech parasite, but we can use it to make crimson dye.

If it's a parasite, then it's fine...

How do you make yellow?

From saffron, for example...

The spice? I love it!

Mixing oil with eggs and saffron to make yellow paint sounds like a cooking recipe...

Hehe, that's true!

Anyway, our chat has helped me realize what I want to be when I grow up...

I'm pleased!

I'm sure you'll make a great painter!

Nah, a great cook!

39

Smiley

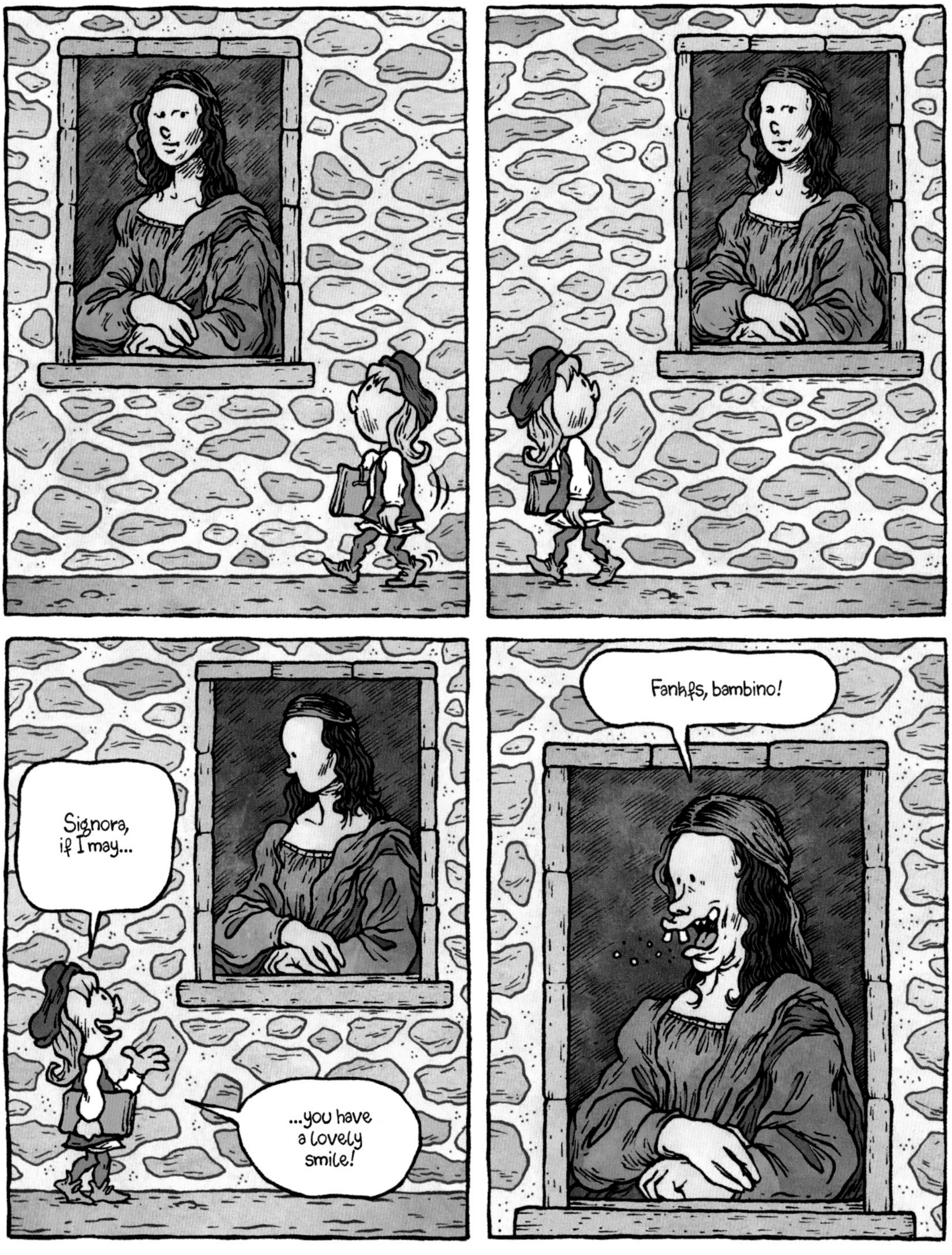
Signora, if I may...
...you have a lovely smile!
Fankfs, bambino!

The Olives

Ugh...this is tiring and repetitive!

Yep, that's olive harvesting for you!

You know I'm thinking about making an olive press?

Oh?

Why not an olive tree shaker while I'm at it?

That'd make things easier, wouldn't it? What do you think?

And what would we do if we get replaced by the machines?

Nothing! That's the best part!

Congratulations!

Thanks!

You just invented unemployment!

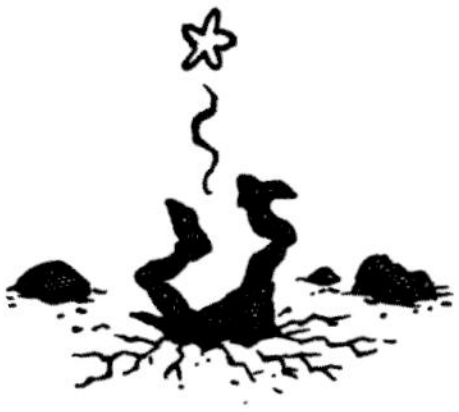

The Big Jump

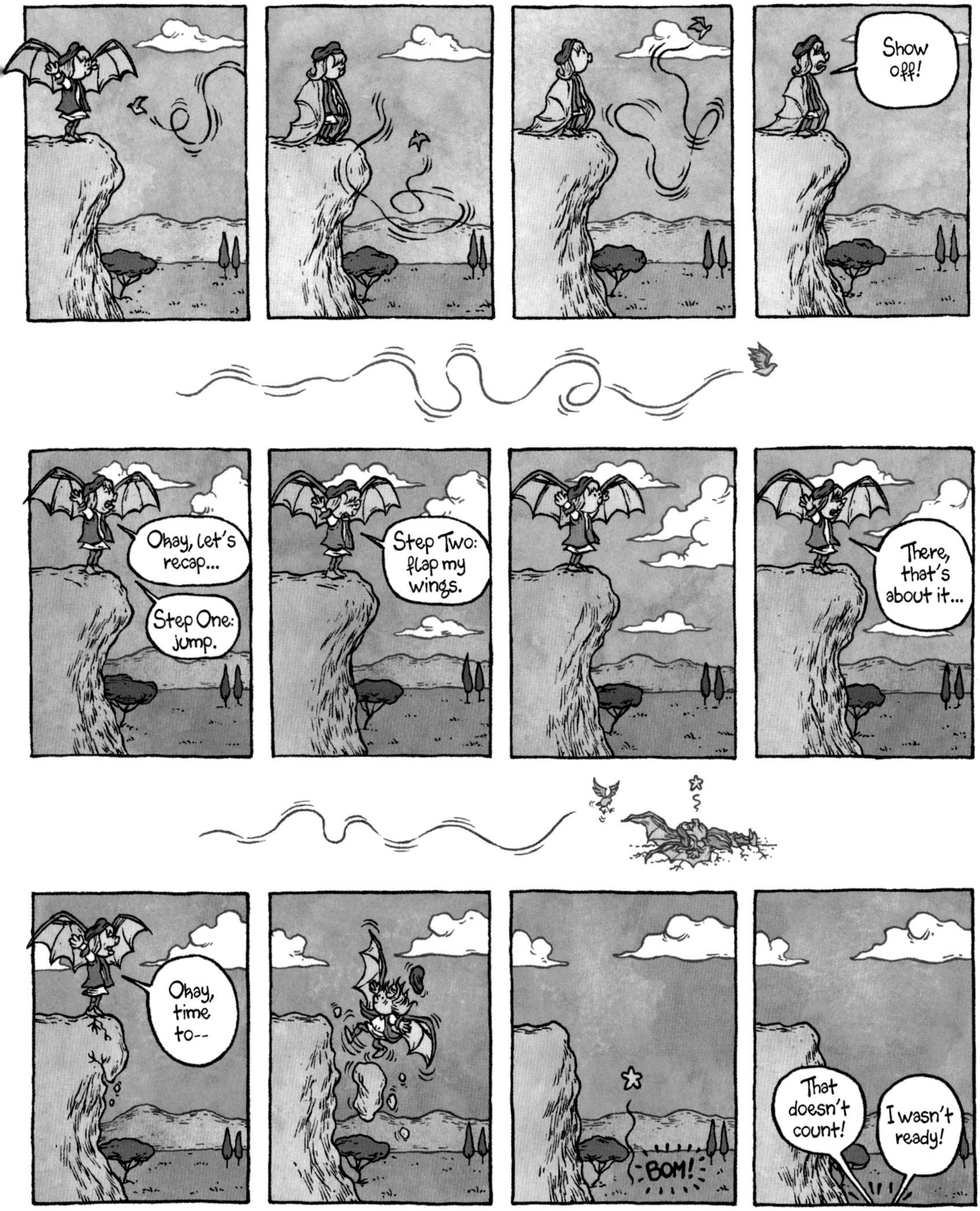

Show off!
Okay, let's recap...
Step One: jump.
Step Two: flap my wings.
There, that's about it...
Okay, time to--
BOM!
That doesn't count!
I wasn't ready!

A dragon?

Yes, a baby dragon, I found it in a cave...

OOoh...

I tamed him, and later on he'll carry me up to the sky!

Do you think he'll be able to breathe fire?

I hope so!

Ha ha! Got ya!

It's just a lizard in disguise!

You shoulda seen your face!

All it took was some string, some paper, and some--

Whatever! Have fun with that...

You have to be really gullible to think a lizard is a...

AAAAH!

The Cage

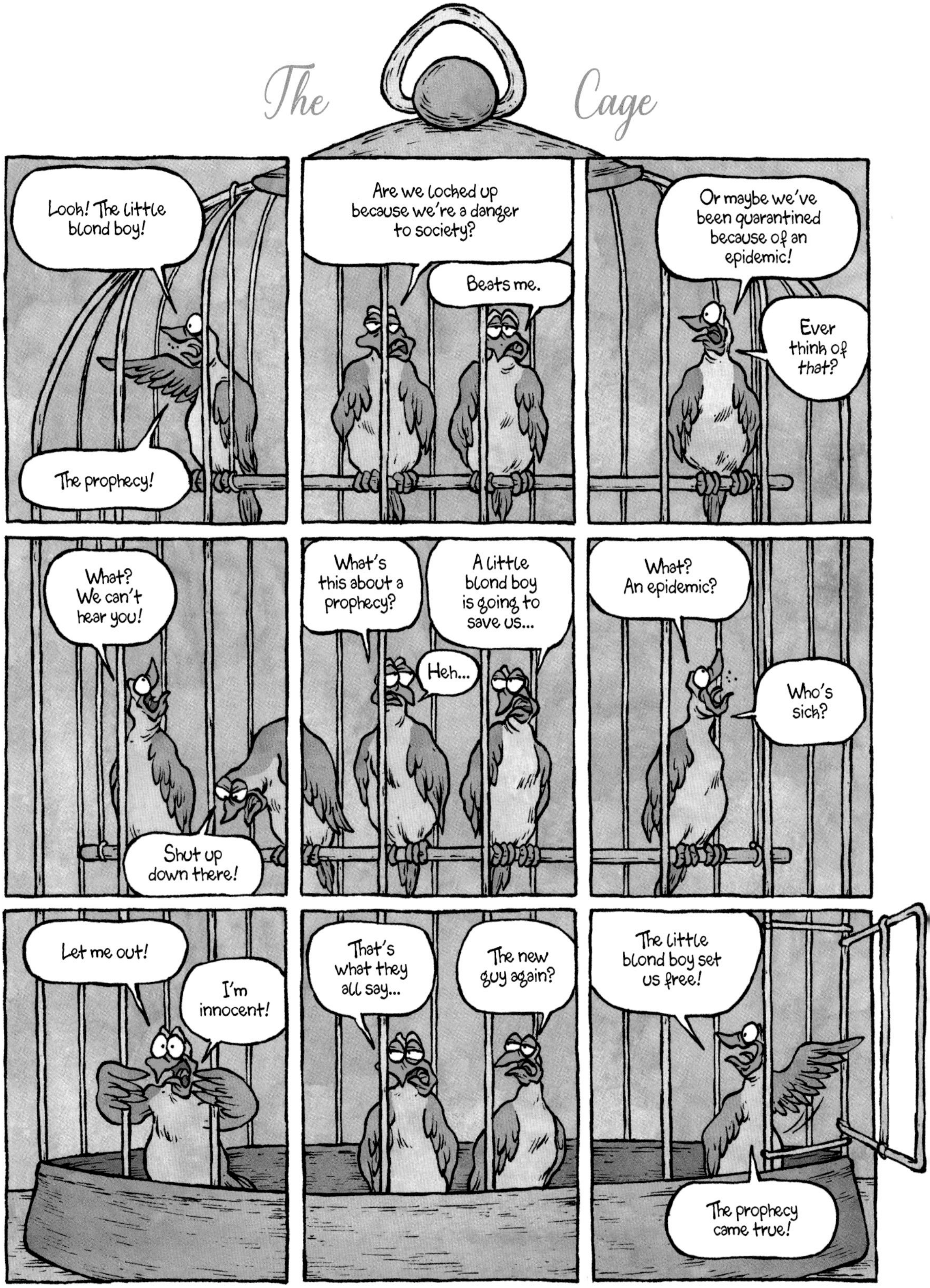
Look! The little blond boy!
The prophecy!
Are we locked up because we're a danger to society?
Beats me.
Or maybe we've been quarantined because of an epidemic!
Ever think of that?
What? We can't hear you!
Shut up down there!
What's this about a prophecy?
A little blond boy is going to save us...
Heh...
What? An epidemic?
Who's sick?
Let me out!
I'm innocent!
That's what they all say...
The new guy again?
The little blond boy set us free!
The prophecy came true!

Meow Cow

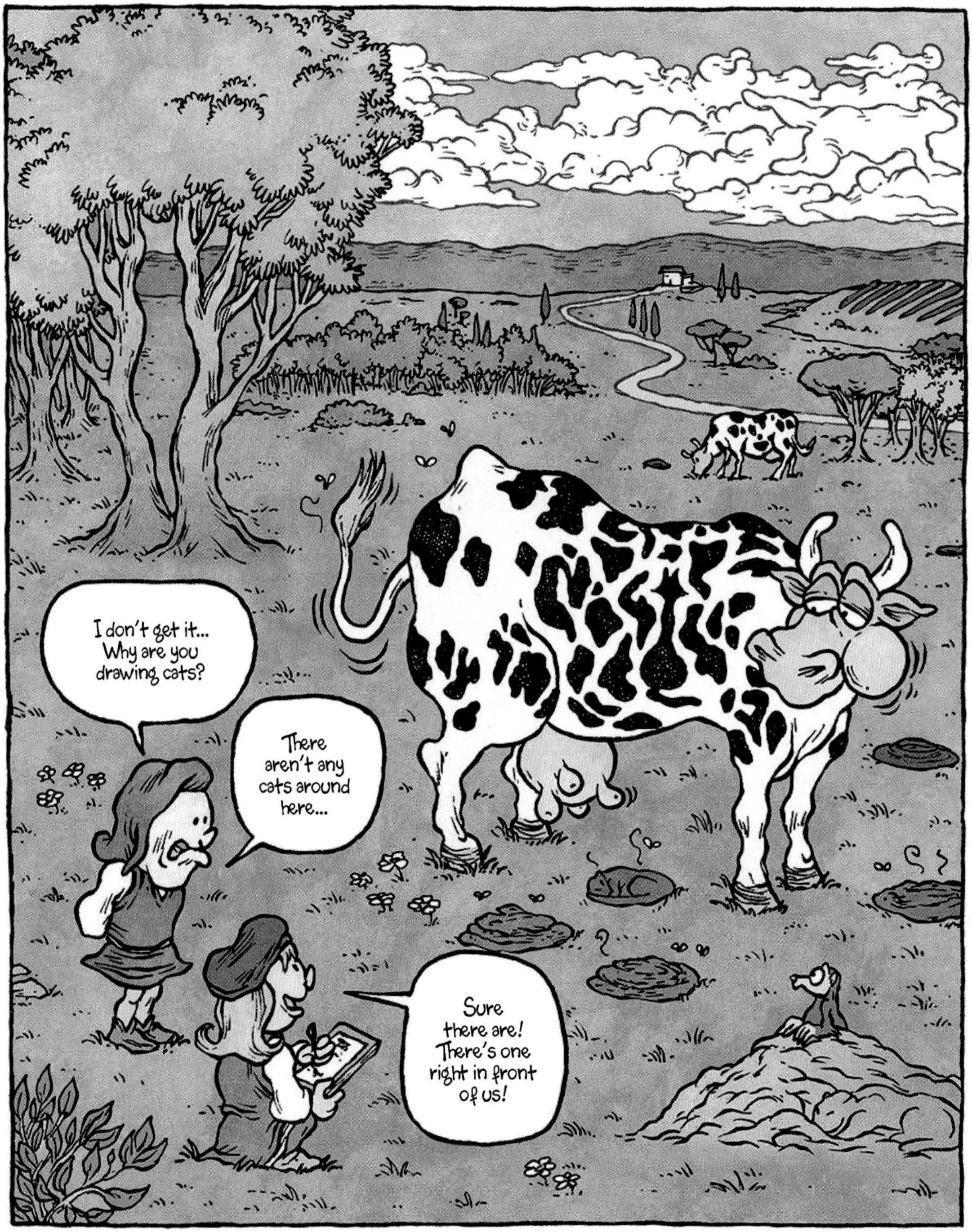

I don't get it... Why are you drawing cats?
There aren't any cats around here...
Sure there are! There's one right in front of us!

The time will come when men
will look upon the research
of animals as they look upon
the research of man.

Leonardo

47

Mario

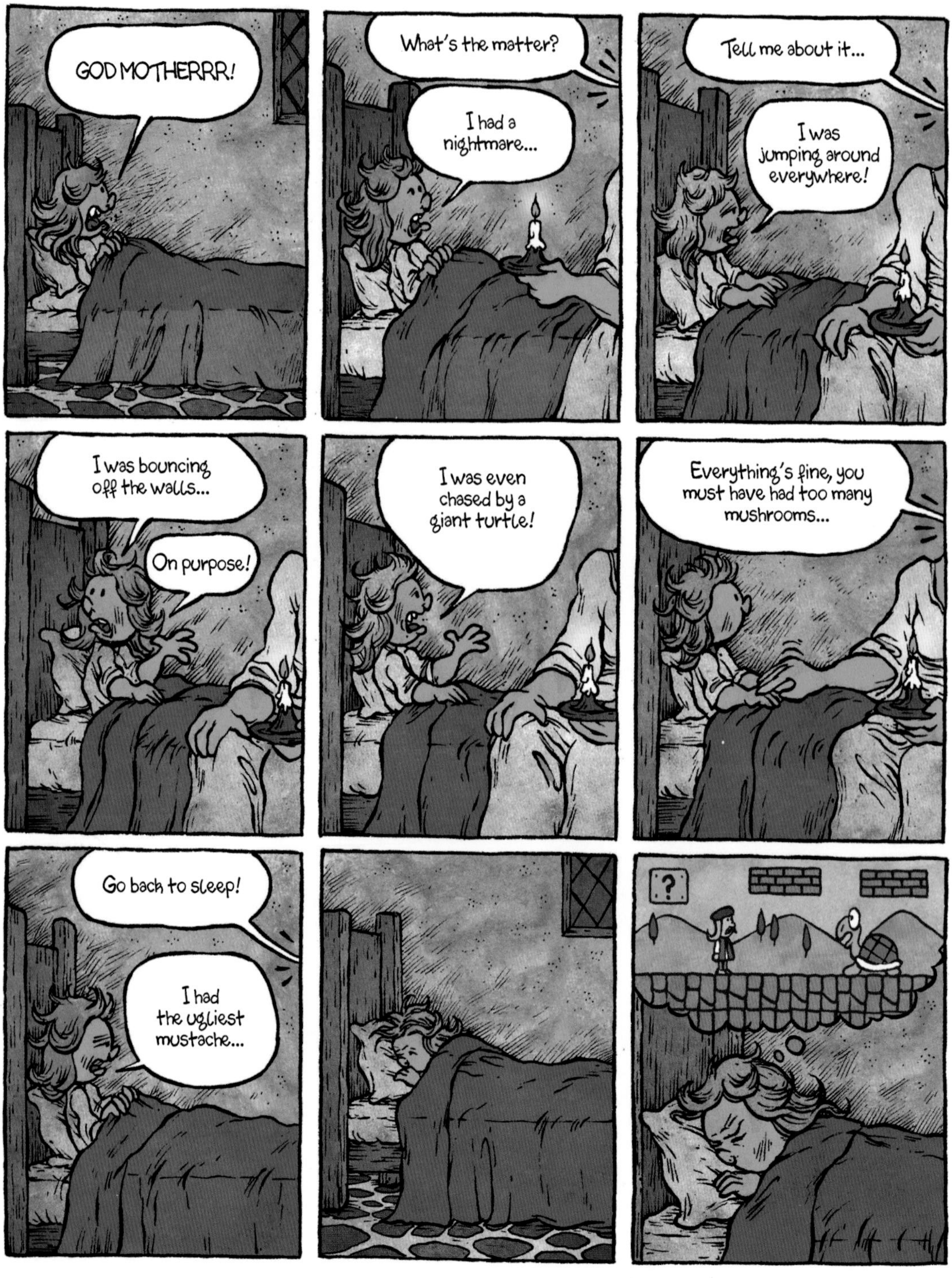
GOD MOTHERRR!
What's the matter?
I had a nightmare...
Tell me about it...
I was jumping around everywhere!
I was bouncing off the walls...
On purpose!
I was even chased by a giant turtle!
Everything's fine, you must have had too many mushrooms...
Go back to sleep!
I had the ugliest mustache...
?

The Smile

What's that?

A sculpture of a laughing woman...

Is she laughing? We can see her teeth, she looks angry...

It looks like she's yelling at us...

...as if we'd done something wrong...

She looks like my mom...

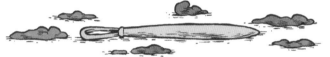

I changed her, now she's just smiling...

Is she smiling? Doesn't look like it...

You should stop making sculptures of smiling women...

It's not your thing!

You should do cats instead...

Everyone loves cats...

Stop smiling!

You're gonna ruin it...

 # The Chair

Ow! My back!

Aahh...

Poor Nonno...

You aren't sitting right...

I know! I'm going to invent a customized chair for you!

Now you just wait and see!

Ow...

First, I have to ask you a few questions...

How much do you weigh?

154 pounds, I think...

I already know how long your legs are...

I measured you while you were napping...

What?

How would you rate the firmness of your rear?

Firm?

Medium firm?

Soft?

Or mushy?

You weren't very cooperative, so I had to get creative...

I need you to sit in this clay to make a print...

There's no way I'm putting my rear in that!

Do it for science!

50

The Chair Part 2

 I still have a couple more questions before I can make the perfect chair!

 I'll cooperate if they aren't all about the size of my tush....

 Very well then, I'll just use my imagination... That's quite alright!

 What if I attached wheels to his chair...

 I could call it a wheelchair! I'm a genius!

 No wheels! I'm old but not disabled!

 Old but with sensitive hearing... That's right!

 There, I'm done, I've taken everything into account...

 You can even recline the backrest... ...thanks to these cogs here...

 This all sounds great! When are you going to build it?

 What? You want me to build it too?

Business As Usual

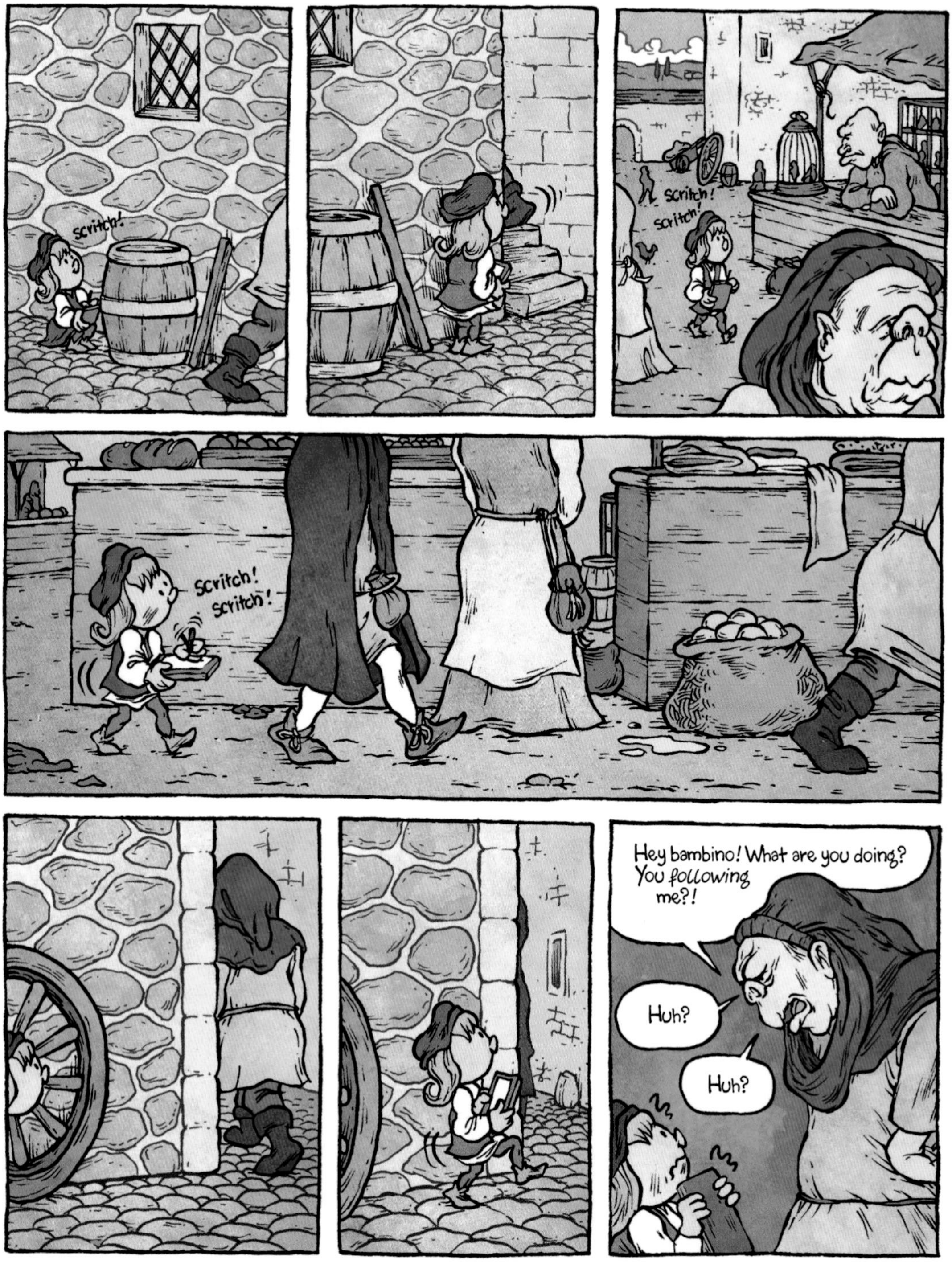
scritch!
Scritch!
Scritch!
Scritch!
Scritch!
Hey bambino! What are you doing? You following me?!
Huh?
Huh?

I... I... no...

I mean, yes, but...

Let me explain...

I follow people who have a certain, uh... appearance, to draw them...

Don't be offended, I deliberately exaggerated your traits...

See for yourself...

Heeheehee! they are a bit exaggerated...

...yet very accurate!

Good work!

It's not like the portraits all those rich people pay for that make them look better...

The rich spend a *fortune* on these portraits...

You know...

...that gives me an *idea*...

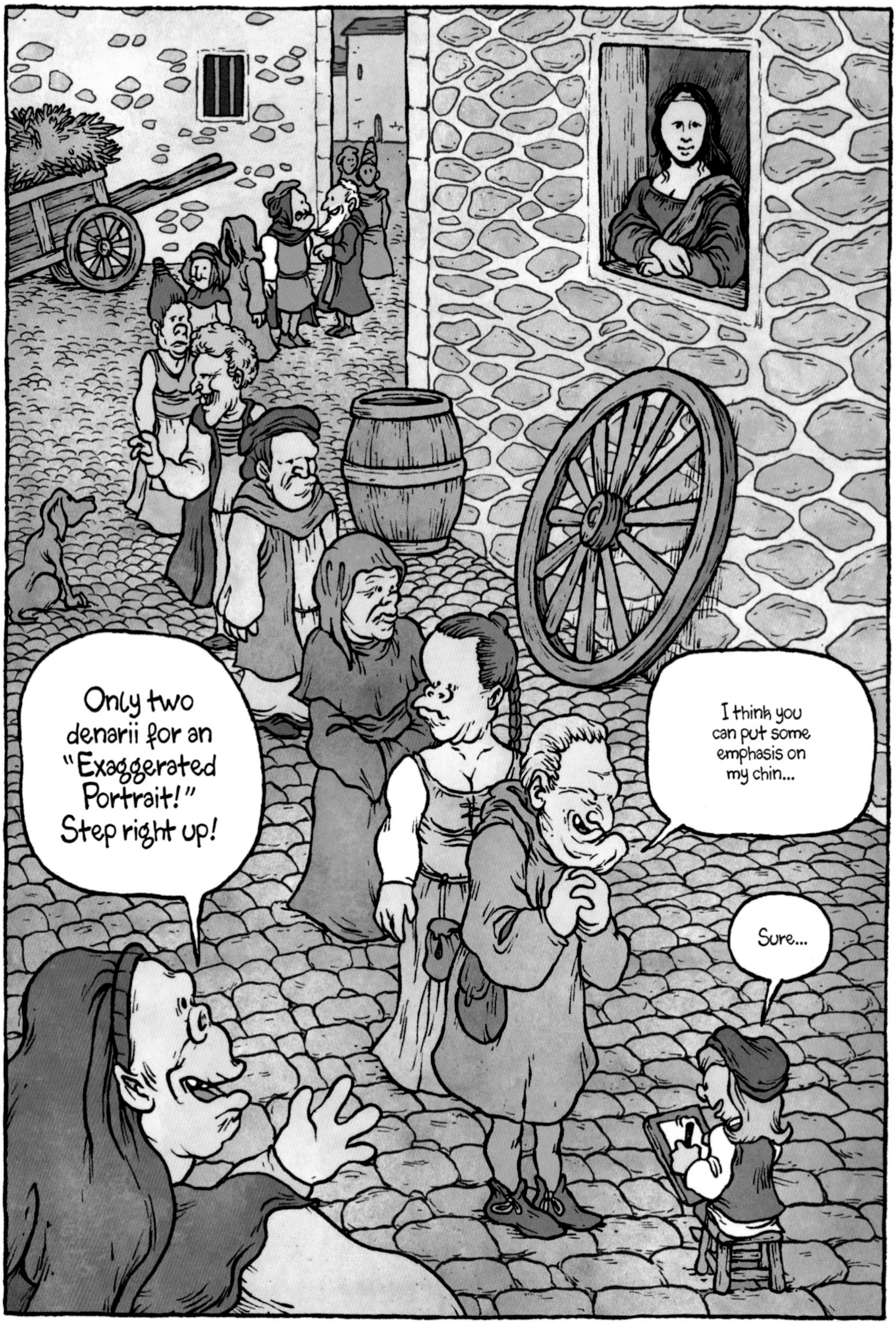

Only two denarii for an "Exaggerated Portrait!" Step right up!
I think you can put some emphasis on my chin...
Sure...

A Small Step. . .

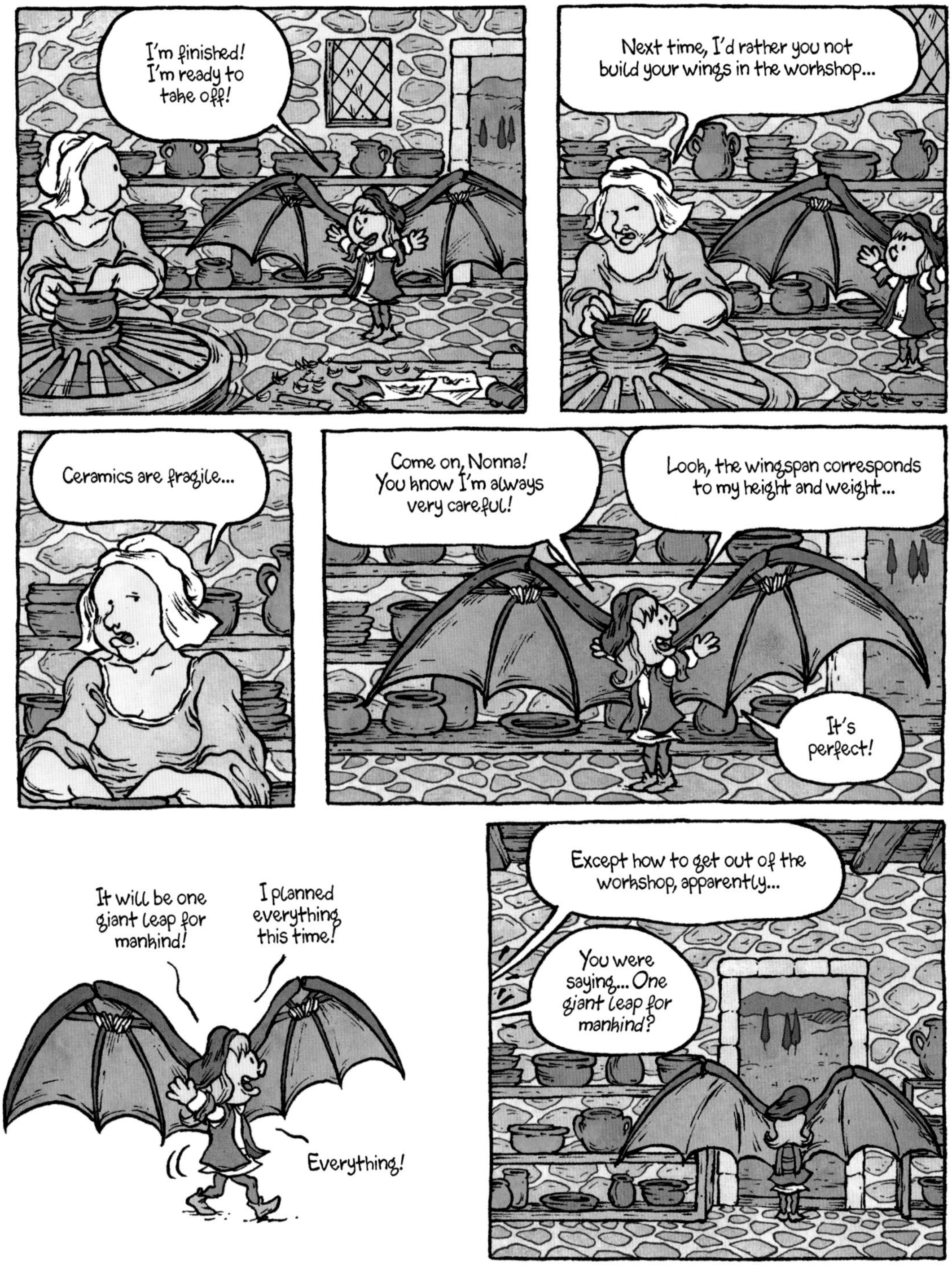
I'm finished! I'm ready to take off!
Next time, I'd rather you not build your wings in the workshop...
Ceramics are fragile...
Come on, Nonna! You know I'm always very careful!
Look, the wingspan corresponds to my height and weight...
It's perfect!
It will be one giant leap for mankind!
I planned everything this time!
Everything!
Except how to get out of the workshop, apparently...
You were saying... One giant leap for mankind?

Motion is the cause of all life.

Leonardo

A Gift From Above

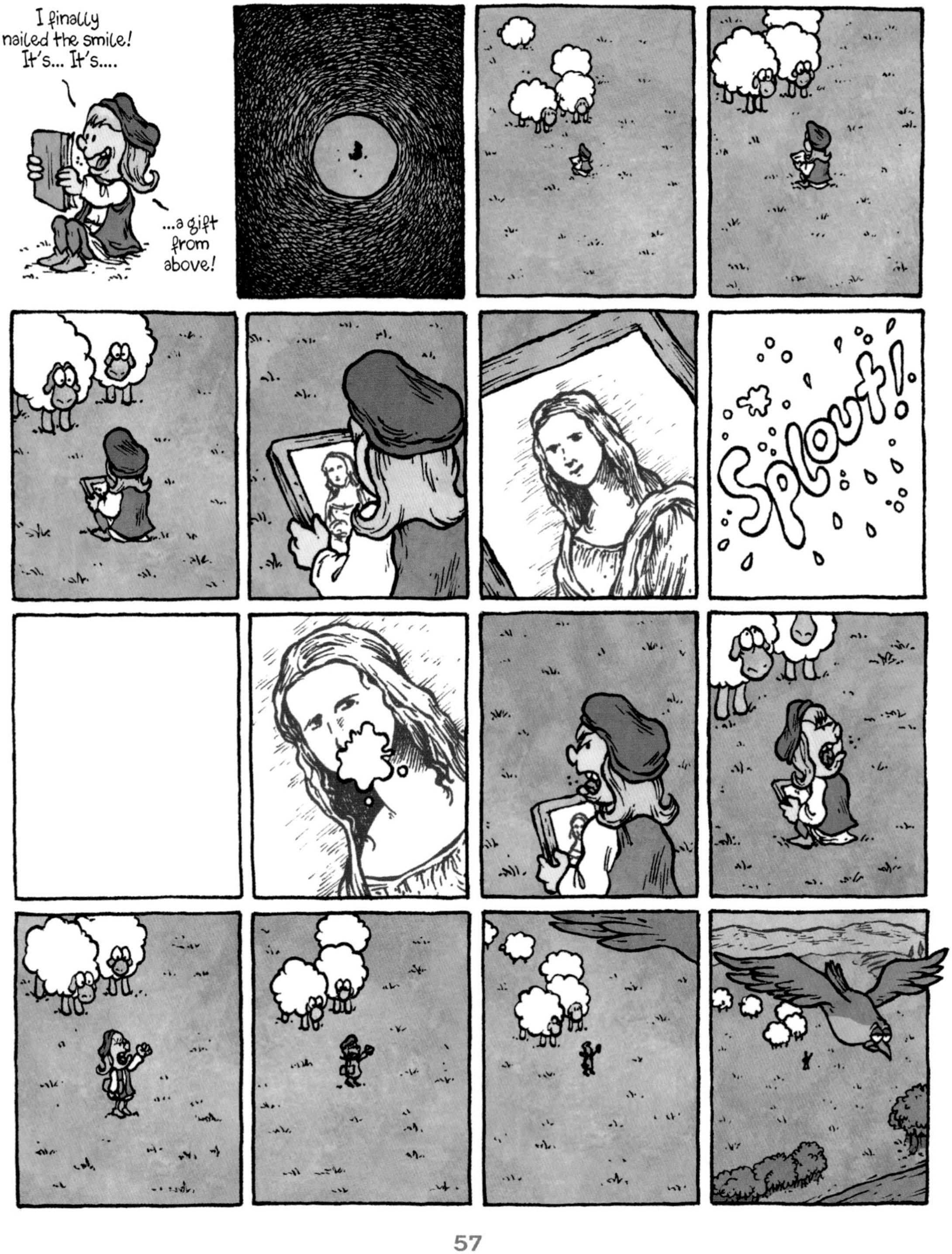
I finally nailed the smile! It's... It's....
...a gift from above!
Splout!

The Ladybug

Are you going to fly? Which animal did you get inspiration from this time?

A bat? An owl? How about a flying fish? Hehehe!

Nope, a ladybug!

HA!
Hey, you look pretty cute!
HA! HA!
HA! HA!
HA!
HA!

HA!
HA! HA!
HA! HA!
HA!
HA!
Pretty cute...

First of all, ladybugs eat aphids for breakfast!

It's a ghastly predator!

HA! HA! HA! HA!
HA! HA! HA!
HA! HA!
HA! HA!
HA!

I should avoid getting up in arms in public...

Dragon Breath

So how's that dragon coming along?

Fine, but I don't have enough clay...

What do you mean, not enough clay?

What... What have you done?

You said I could make a dragon...

Represent a dragon on pottery!

Oh...

Besides, it's too big to bake in the oven...

Oh...

Unless it can breath fire to cook itself...

I don't see how you're going to deal with that...

Cook itself?

Nonna, that's genius!

If I use its belly as a hearth...

...and connect a pipe to its mouth, I...

Come on, Leo, I was kidding!

That's ridiculous!

What's next, making it fly?

Making it fly? That's even more genius!

Of course, this would require gigantic wings...

Hmm...

I give up...

That's it, a big canvas...

We should not desire
the impossible.
Leonardo

61

Friends

Hey Goldilocks, when you gettin' a haircut?

Yeah, you look like a girl!

Reprove your friend in secret...

...and praise him in public.

He talks like a girl, too!

Yeah, hehe!

If by that, you mean I speak like a human being... then yes, you are correct.

62

The Creature From the Lagoon

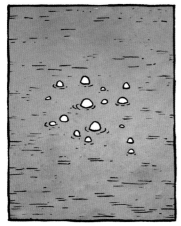

You fools, I was just asking you to help me...

I was suffocating...

Oh no! It ate Leo!

And it was suffocating him!

HAAAAAA

HAAAAAA

The world isn't ready for underwater diving...

Floaties

Paolo, are you going to the lake?

Uh, yeah...

You wanna try out one of my floating devices?

Is... Is it dangerous?

On the contrary! You wear it around your waist to keep from sinking!

The first one is made of cork oak...

A very lightweight material!

The second one is an inflated cow rumen...

Which one would you like to try?

A rumen, is that the cow's stomach?

That's right!

In other words, the cow's poop pouch?

That's right!

You want the cork oak one, don't you?

Duh.

Perfection

What a noble animal, such harmonious curves!

To draw it well, you have to focus on every detail...

Details make perfection, and perfection is not a detail...

That's *brilliant!* I'll write that down!

Details make perfection...

..and perfection is not a detail...

...depends on the detail...

The Milky Way

The sun is what lights up the moon...

Did you know that?

And if it shines so bright, it's because there's water...

There's got to be...

What do you see when you look at the moon, Signore Gatto?

I'll bet you see a big bowl of milk...

...and it splatters all around into stars...

Hehe!

That bowl of milk would be hard to reach...

...but I could probably make you a long straw...

Ciao, Nonno!

So you're headed off to Florence?

Yeah...

You're going to learn how to paint with a master!

Yeah, yeah...

You don't look very happy...

It's not that...

I just don't want to leave you, Nonno!

Leo, I belong here, but you've got the whole world to explore...

Cheer up, you have so much to discover!

And what is it I always say?

Keep...*sniff* your...eyes...open!

Promise me you'll always keep your eyes open?

I promise...

...once they've dried.

Goodbye Gift

What's this? A letter...

Who could it be from?

I'm sorry for all the trouble I've caused you, here's the portrait I promised you.

Leonardo

promised you. Leonardo

Bandito...

Dear Nonna,

I was never able to draw the flowers the way you wanted...

but assuming they're simple geometric patterns, I solved the problem. With much love,

Leonardo

Ooh... Leonardo...

Dear Paolo,

I am offering you my new catapult as a present. To use it, stand in front of it and pull the lever. Enjoy!

Leonardo

Stand in front...

...and pull the lever.

Ow!

Goldilocks!

70

I hope you're proud to join Master Verrochio's studio...

You bet!

Now I can do all the things I've always dreamed of doing!

That's just it, no more dreaming...

You have too much of a tendency to start things and never finish them...

Mmm...

You've spread yourself too thin!

It's time for you to learn from a great master...

Mmm...

Learn what, for example?

Sculpture?

Painting?

Plaster work?

Metallurgy?

Leather work?

Mechanics?

Hmm...

Geometry?

Chemistry?

The painter has
the universe in his mind
and hands.

Leonardo

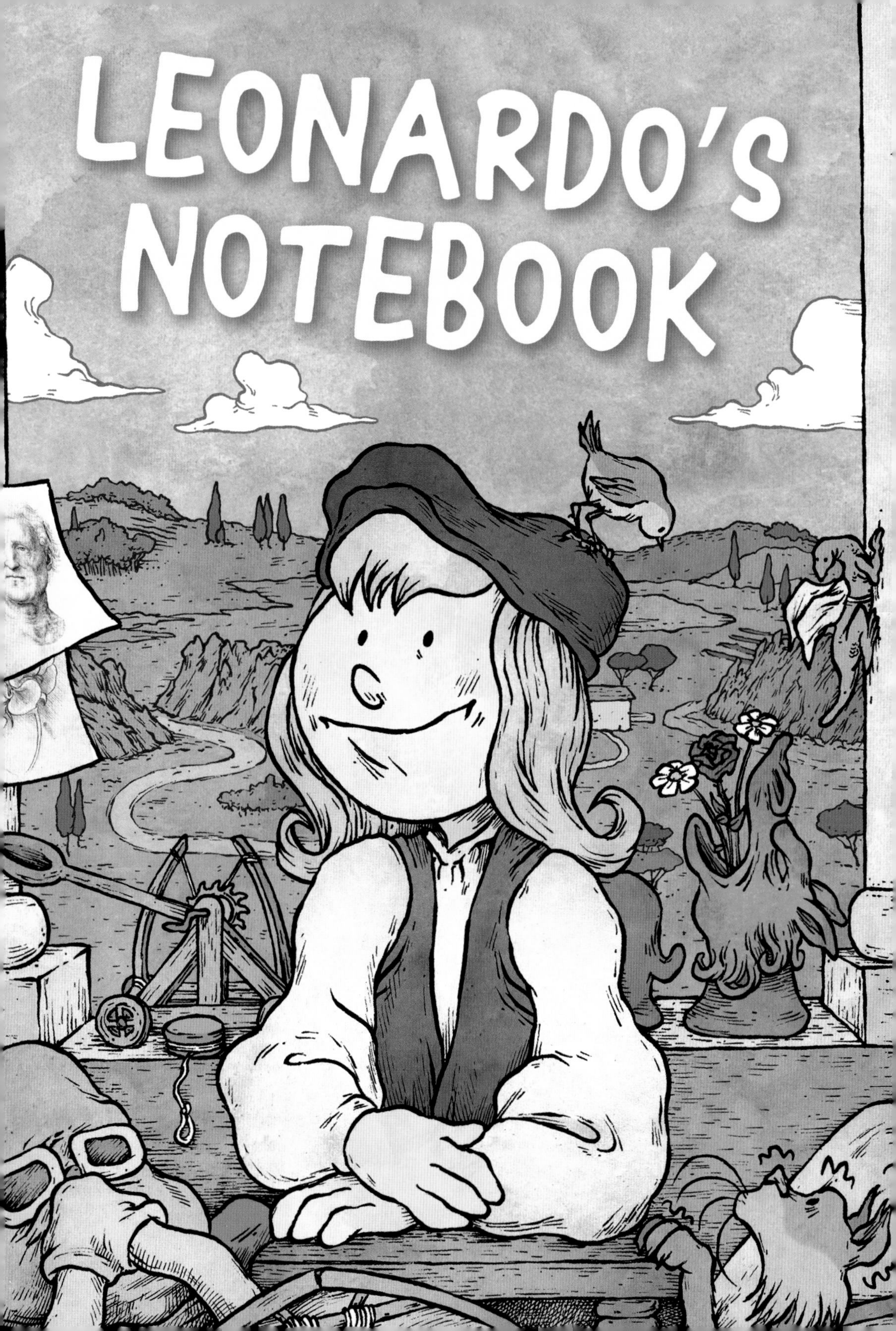
LEONARDO'S
NOTEBOOK

WHO WAS LEONARDO DA VINCI?

🦇 Leonardo da Vinci was born on April 15, 1452 in Tuscany, near Florence, Italy.

🦇 He had 12 brothers and sisters.

🦇 Leonardo wasn't just an artist, but a mathematician, scientist, writer, musician, and inventor.

🦇 He wrote over 6,000 pages in his personal journals... backward!

Hi! I'm Leonardo da Vinci. If you can read this, you must be very clever!

When Leonardo was just 14 years old, he became a ***garzone*** (someone who helps out artists in their studios) for Verrocchio, who was one of the most famous painters and sculptors in Florence at the time.

Leonardo was **ambidextrous**, which meant he could write with both his left and right hands.

He is known as a **Renaissance Man**, or someone who has great talent and knowledge in many areas.

Leonardo invented the first **armored car** and **scuba diving suit**.

He was a **vegetarian**! He would often buy caged birds so that he could set them free.

Did you know that Leonardo da Vinci invented the first ever parachute? Now it's your turn!

Follow the instructions to create your very own!

WHAT YOU'LL NEED:

Plastic bag

Scissors

Ruler

String

Rock

INSTRUCTIONS:

1. Cut out a large square from your plastic bag, around 10 inches in length.

2. Cut off the corners of the square so it looks like an octagon (a shape with 8 sides).

3. Cut a small hole near the edge of each side.

4. Cut 8 pieces of string, each around 12 inches long.

5. Attach the 8 strings to each of the holes.

6. Tie all the ends of the string to the object you are using as a weight.

7. Find a safe, high spot to drop your parachute from and **see how well it works!**

PLAY WITH LEONARDO

QUIZ YOURSELF

1 PROCRASTINATION

2 BAMBINO

3 FASCINATING

4 GENIUS

5 PATAGIA

6 BUONGIORNO

7 CIAO

**Uh-Oh, Leonardo is at it again!
Help him release the caged birds by pairing
each word with its correct definition.**

A. "Good morning" in Italian.

B. The action of delaying or postponing something, or putting it off until the last minute.

C. The folds of skin between the forelimbs of a bat, or any other mammal, that help them to glide.

D. Extremely interesting.

E. Someone who has exceptional intelligence, creativity, or natural talent.

F. "Child" in Italian.

G. Italian for both "hello" and "goodbye."

ANSWER KEY- 1-B, 2-F, 3-D, 4-E, 5-C, 6-A, 7-G

NONNAS BROKEN POTS

1.

A.

2.

B.

3.

C.

4.

D.

5.

E.

Oh no! It looks like Leo broke all 5 of Nonna's pots! Help him put them back together by matching the numbered halves to the correct lettered halves!

ANSWER KEY: 1-E, 2-D, 3-B, 4-A, 5-C

OVERVIEW

Fiction meets art history in the playful and imaginative graphic novel *Young Leonardo* by William Augel. Told through a series of short fictional comics about Leonardo da Vinci's childhood, the book introduces readers to young Leonardo as a precocious, curious, and talented kid still living at home with his family in Italy. The vignettes follow Leonardo as he shows off his newest inventions, conducts experiments, creates art, and studies the world—both to the admiration and frustration of his neighbors and family—on his path to future greatness.

Though the stories and Leonardo's interests vary widely, together they reveal a young boy fascinated with the world around him, one who is destined to become one of the most renowned artists and thinkers of all-time. By mixing fiction and humor with real anecdotes and characters from Leonardo da Vinci's life, *Young Leonardo* provides a unique and relatable perspective on this larger-than-life figure for young readers.

CHARACTERS

Nonna

Leonardo
da Vinci

Francesco
da Vinci

Nonno

Salvatore

Albiera
degli Amadori

Paolo

Piero
da Vinci

Signore
Gatto

Andrea del
Verrocchio

Leonardo da Vinci is the main character and protagonist of *Young Leonardo*. An inquisitive and often irreverent kid, Leonardo is constantly creating, experimenting, and thinking about new ways to improve his life and the world around him. His interests are seemingly infinite but include hobbies like painting, sculpting, flight, exploration, anatomy, and much more, giving readers a small window into just how multi-talented and influential Leonardo will eventually become in real life.

"Nonno" Antonio da Vinci is Leonardo's grandfather. He often encourages Leonardo to create new inventions, but with mixed results. He also tries to give Leonardo some much-needed wisdom in order to temper his more careless impulses.

"Nonna" Lucia di Zoso is Leonardo's grandmother. Usually found in her ceramics studio, she sometimes calls on Leonardo for help creating and painting pottery, though they are rarely in agreement as to what "help" actually entails.

Francesco da Vinci is Leonardo's uncle. The outdoorsman and farmer of the family, he teaches Leonardo about things like food, animals, and other aspects of the natural world.

Piero da Vinci and Albiera degli Amadori are Leonardo's father and godmother, respectively. Their characters are rarely seen throughout the book.

Andrea del Verrocchio is Leonardo's real-life future mentor. In the graphic novel, Andrea serves as Leonardo's artistic inspiration, helping to answer Leonardo's many questions about how and why to create different kinds of art.

Paolo is known as "The Lout." He is usually found helping Leonardo with one of his schemes…or being the unwitting victim of one.

Salvatore is known as "The Bird Merchant" and owns a pet shop in the city near where Leonardo lives. Despite his best efforts, Salvatore's birds are constantly being set free by Leonardo, a proud vegetarian and animal lover.

Signore Gatto is Leonardo's cat. He can often be found spending time alone with Leonardo and listening to musings about life, poetry, nature, the universe, and whatever else is on his mind. He is afraid of birds!

SETTINGS

Leonardo's Family Home is where he attempts to balance family life and expectations with his pursuit of knowledge. When he's not spending time with his family, Leonardo is usually inventing something new, studying, or scheming for his next big project.

The Outdoors is where Leonardo performs many of his experiments, explores new worlds, and creates new art. From caves to pastures to lakes to snowy hills, Leonardo's travels take him and the occasional family member into new challenges and discoveries.

The City provides Leonardo a place to interact with other people in spots such as the local pet shop or public marketplace. Drawn in a 15th-century, quaint Italian style complete with cobblestone streets, the city is where Leonardo goes with the goal of selling or testing some new idea with a larger audience.

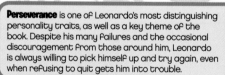

THEMES

Creativity and Passion for art and science are something that many of the book's characters, especially Leonardo, exhibit throughout *Young Leonardo*. Leonardo's interests in painting, sculpting, drawing, flight, math, writing, space, agriculture, and even bridge-building, among many others, are the driving force behind almost all his decisions. As he tests out new ideas and experiments, readers also have the opportunity to see snapshots of real-life Leonardo da Vinci's future creations.

Pride and Ego are traits that Leonardo exhibits in various ways throughout the book. Portrayed sometimes as a know-it-all, Leonardo's failures are often due to being overly self-confident in an idea or action despite the risks and consequences. However, his successful ideas and inventions also show the power of having confidence and pride in one's work.

Perseverance is one of Leonardo's most distinguishing personality traits, as well as a key theme of the book. Despite his many failures and the occasional discouragement from those around him, Leonardo is always willing to pick himself up and try again, even when refusing to quit gets him into trouble.

Family is the foundation of almost all the relationships in Young Leonardo. Leonardo's very large family provides an essential support system, both for his ideas and for his physical well-being, which helps him feel comfortable to take risks and be creative. This theme is most apparent in the relationships between Leonardo and his grandparents.

Dreams and Ambition show up in various ways, both literally and figuratively. While Leonardo literally dreams about his inventions being a success, he also aspires to master multiple art forms and sciences as a young child. His irrepressible ambition and curiosity give readers similar permission to chase after their own passions no matter what they might be.

PRE READING IDEAS

1. Have students write or discuss what they know about Leonardo da Vinci, or provide them with a quick overview of da Vinci's life and notable achievements. Note that very little information exists on da Vinci's childhood life and ask them: What do they think Leonardo would have been like as a child? What things might he have been able to do that others couldn't? And what might he have struggled with that others didn't?

2. Have students answer the prompt: If you could invent anything, what would it be? Encourage them to think about a problem in the world or their communities that this invention would solve. As a follow-up, provide them examples of Leonardo da Vinci's inventions and ask them what they think about what problems he may have been trying to solve when creating them.

3. Have students quickly scan through the text of the graphic novel for words they do not recognize. Students should keep a list of these words, then use a dictionary to look up the definitions of the words. The teacher or students can compile the most commonly unrecognized words into a companion document that students can reference while reading. Students might find it extra helpful if the companion document is divided into English and Italian words.

DISCUSSION QUESTIONS

1. Leonardo is often helping his family with projects or planning his own at home. What kind of relationship do you think Leonardo has with each of his family members? How can you tell? Provide specific examples from the text as well as the images.

2. Why do you think Leonardo dislikes sports so much?

3. Why do you think Leonardo sometimes gets bullied and teased by other kids? How does he handle these situations? Do you see any examples in the book where Leonardo bullies or teases others, even unintentionally?

4. Why do you think Leonardo tries to write in his journal backwards? What does this show about his character?

5. Often Leonardo's inventions don't work as he expects, such as his many failed experiments with flying. Why do you think he keeps trying over and over again? Why is this important to him? How does this relate to what you know about Leonardo da Vinci as an adult?

6. In the story "Pigments," Leonardo learns about color. Look at the use of specific colors throughout the book to represent characters and settings. What do you notice? Why do you think the artist chose this style of art? How does it enhance the reading experience?

7. In the story "Icarus," Nonno tells Leonardo the story of Icarus and Daedalus. While Leonardo draws his own conclusions about the myth, Nonno was clearly trying to impart a different message. What message from the story of Icarus do you think Nonno was trying to present?

8. The book ends with Leonardo leaving for Florence, Italy. How are these final few stories different from those in the rest of the book? Does it change the way you feel about Leonardo and/or his family? If so, why?

9. What do you think will happen to Leonardo when he gets to Florence?

10. Many of the stories in *Young Leonardo* are based on some aspect of Leonardo da Vinci's real life. Why do you think the author did this? What do you think is the larger goal of this book and presenting Leonardo da Vinci in this way?

11. What can you infer about the character Leonardo da Vinci and his importance to history from the stories in Young Leonardo?

12. Some stories are only four panels long, while others take place over a few pages. Why do you think the writer decided to make some stories longer and some shorter? What different types of techniques do you notice cross over between stories?
How do the different lengths of the stories change your experience reading them? Provide specific examples.

PROJECT IDEAS

Wordless Comic: Have them compare the comics in *Young Leonardo* that include text with those that do not include text. What do students notice about the differences between each? Give students a simple story, then ask them to create a wordless comic that tells this story using only images. For inspiration, consider having students write the next story in the book, when Leonardo arrives in Florence, without words. For an added challenge, students can work to incorporate humor into their wordless comic.

Create a Quote: Sprinkled throughout *Young Leonardo* are quotes from the real Leonardo da Vinci meant to add an additional layer of context or an inspirational takeaway. Assign each student a story, then have students create their own motto/tagline to go with it that captures the larger lesson/moral of the story. For contemporary reference materials, consider using movie posters or trailers as examples. Have students present their quote to the class and explain, with specific examples, how it connects to the story they selected.

Humor Comic: Many of the stories throughout *Young Leonardo* are built in a Sunday-comic style joke format with a clear set-up and punchline. Have students select which story in the book they find the most humorous. Then, have students provide specific examples of where the author used images and/or text to create humor, and why. Once they've analyzed their chosen story, students should draw inspiration from their own childhood antics and create a short comic using this same format to tell a joke or depict a humorous situation. Their comic should use a mix of text and images.

Mechanics of Flight: Leonardo da Vinci was fascinated with the properties and physics of flight, both in this graphic novel and in real life. In this activity, create a simple wind tunnel with a small home fan and plastic or cardboard. Students can learn about lift by creating their own paper aircrafts and seeing how high they can get theirs to float. As an alternative, students can create two paper airplanes with different designs and compare how the designs affects their flight. Measure for distance and accuracy, then allow students to modify one of the aircraft to improve its flight path.

Inventor's Corner: Leonardo da Vinci was a world-famous inventor and one of the leading thinkers of all time. In small groups, have students work together to create and pitch a new invention to help the world. They will need to create a mock-up/drawing of their invention, write a short "pitch" for it, and present it as a group to the class. This project-based learning activity can be enhanced in various ways, such as by assigning students different specialized roles within their group, having students create a print advertisement or short commercials for their invention, or even a presentation to real-life designers and manufacturers.

Self Portrait: Leonardo da Vinci created many pieces of well-known art which include his self-portrait drawn with red chalk on paper. Using a mirror, have students draw their own self-portrait using a medium of the teacher's or students' choosing. After completing their self-portrait, have students reflect upon their experience through writing. What did they notice or learn about themselves during the process? What did they find easy or difficult about drawing their own portrait? How does creating a self-portrait differ from taking inspiration from other real-life objects or their imaginations?

COMMON CORE CONNECTIONS

The reading of this book in combination with a thoughtful analysis through writing, presentation, or discussion (such as the projects within this guide), can promote the teaching or reinforcement of the following Common Core Standards for grades 3-5 found within the Reading: Literature strands, as well as various standards within the Reading; Foundational Skills, Writing, Speaking & Listening; and Language strands for relevant grade levels.

CCSS.ELA-LITERACY.RL.3.1 - Ask and answer questions to demonstrate understanding of a text, referring explicitly to the text as the basis for the answers.
CCSS.ELA-LITERACY.RL.3.2 - Recount stories, including fables, folktales, and myths from diverse cultures; determine the central message, lesson, or moral and explain how it is conveyed through key details in the text.
CCSS.ELA-LITERACY.RL.3.3 - Describe characters in a story (e.g., their traits, motivations, or feelings) and explain how their actions contribute to the sequence of events.
CCSS.ELA-LITERACY.RL.3.4 - Determine the meaning of words and phrases as they are used in a text, distinguishing literal from nonliteral language.
CCSS.ELA-LITERACY.RL.3.5 - Refer to parts of stories, dramas, and poems when writing or speaking about a text, using terms such as chapter, scene, and stanza; describe how each successive part builds on earlier sections.
CCSS.ELA-LITERACY.RL.3.6 - Distinguish their own point of view from that of the narrator or those of the characters.
CCSS.ELA-LITERACY.RL.3.7 - Explain how specific aspects of a text's illustrations contribute to what is conveyed by the words in a story (e.g., create mood, emphasize aspects of a character or setting).
CCSS.ELA-LITERACY.RL.4.1 - Refer to details and examples in a text when explaining what the text says explicitly and when drawing inferences from the text.
CCSS.ELA-LITERACY.RL.4.2 - Determine a theme of a story, drama, or poem from details in the text; summarize the text.
CCSS.ELA-LITERACY.RL.4.3 - Describe in depth a character, setting, or event in a story or drama, drawing on specific details in the text (e.g., a character's thoughts, words, or actions).
CCSS.ELA-LITERACY.RL.4.4 - Determine the meaning of words and phrases as they are used in a text, including those that allude to significant characters found in mythology (e.g., Herculean).
CCSS.ELA-LITERACY.RL.5.1 - Quote accurately from a text when explaining what the text says explicitly and when drawing inferences from the text.
CCSS.ELA-LITERACY.RL.5.2 - Determine a theme of a story, drama, or poem from details in the text, including how characters in a story or drama respond to challenges or how the speaker in a poem reflects upon a topic; summarize the text.
CCSS.ELA-LITERACY.RL.5.3 - Compare and contrast two or more characters, settings, or events in a story or drama, drawing on specific details in the text (e.g., how characters interact).
CCSS.ELA-LITERACY.RL.5.5 - Explain how a series of chapters, scenes, or stanzas fits together to provide the overall structure of a particular story, drama, or poem.
CCSS.ELA-LITERACY.RL.5.7 - Analyze how visual and multimedia elements contribute to the meaning, tone, or beauty of a text (e.g., graphic novel, multimedia presentation of fiction, folktale, myth, poem).
CCSS.ELA-LITERACY.RL.5.9 - Compare and contrast stories in the same genre (e.g., mysteries and adventure stories) on their approaches to similar themes and topics.

FURTHER READINGS

- *Leonardo da Vinci Timeline* (National Geographic Kids)
- *Where Are You, Leopold?* (graphic novel)
- *Young Mozart* (graphic novel)
- *Bigby Bear* (graphic novel))
- *Strega Nona* (picture book)
- *Who Was Leonardo da Vinci?* (book)
- *Amazing Leonardo da Vinci Inventions: You Can Build Yourself* (book)
- *The Time Warp Trio* (book series)

CREATED BY
POP CULTURE
CLASSROOM

FOR FURTHER QUESTIONS, please contact
Harley Salbacka, Sales Representative
harley.salbacka@humanoids.com

BiG 10+

ENCOURAGING YOUNG READERS TO THINK

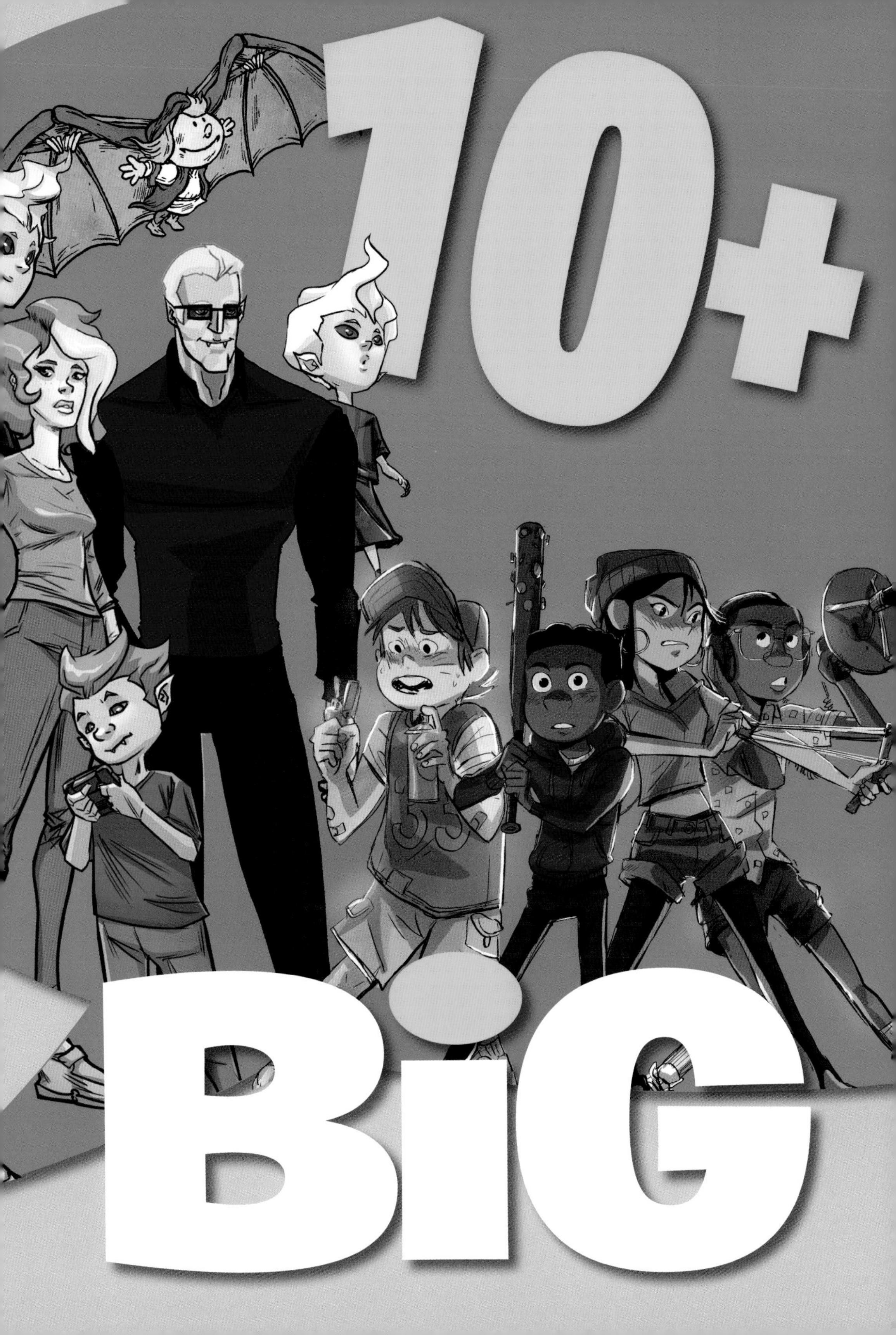
10+
BiG

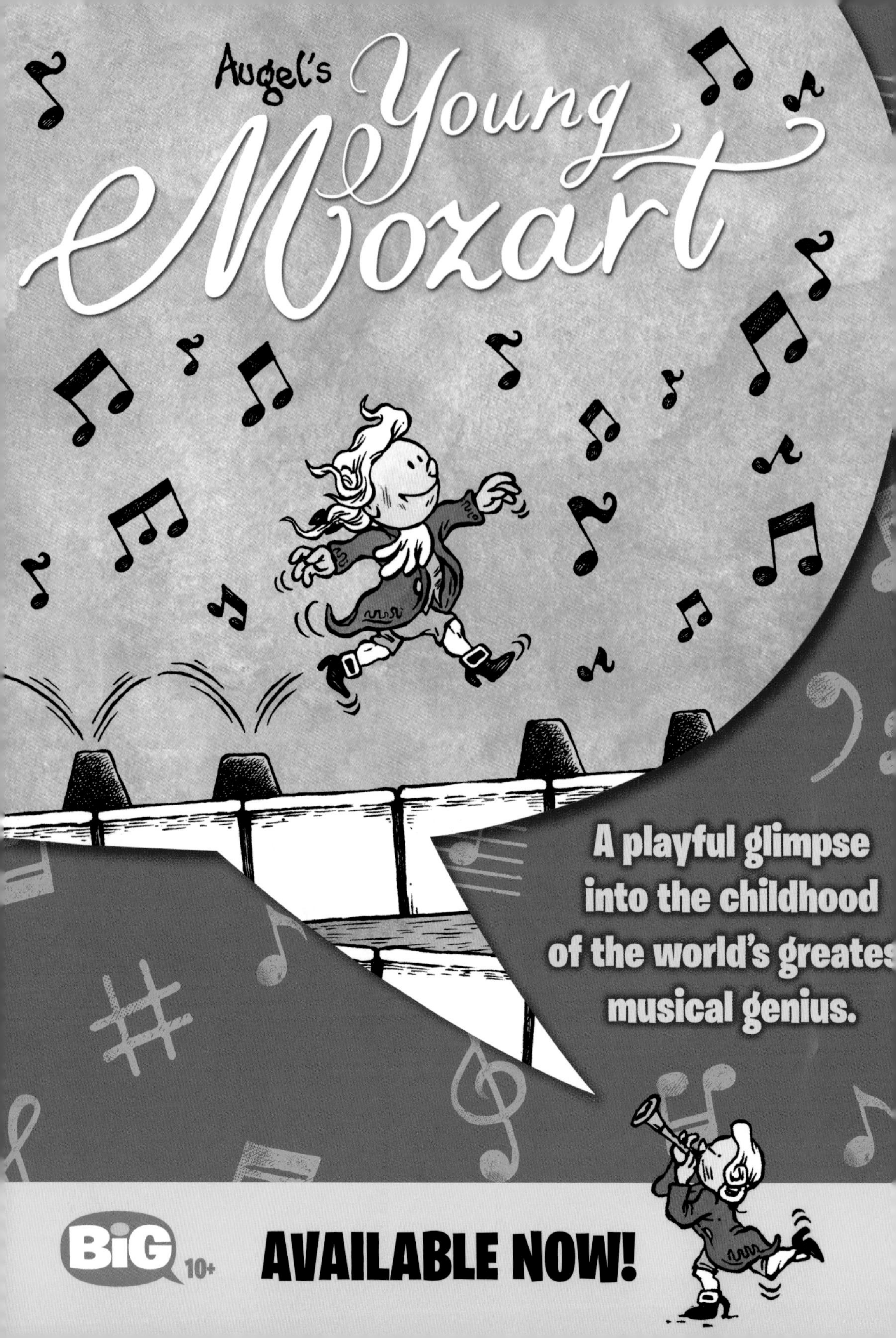
Augel's
Young Mozart
A playful glimpse
into the childhood
of the world's greates
musical genius.
BiG 10+
AVAILABLE NOW!